Voices
in the
MIST

Best Wishes.

Voices
in the
MIST

J. S. RALPH

authorHOUSE®

AuthorHouse™ UK Ltd.
1663 Liberty Drive
Bloomington, IN 47403 USA
www.authorhouse.co.uk
Phone: 0800.197.4150

Published by AuthorHouse 01/03/2014

ISBN: 978-1-4918-8423-2 (sc)
ISBN: 978-1-4918-7856-9 (hc)
ISBN: 978-1-4918-8424-9 (e)

Dear Friend,

The tale I am about to tell you contains information of such magnitude that you will not know whether to believe it or dismiss it.

The setting is real, the story hard to believe. I have given it much thought, and I'm not taking the step to tell this story lightly. After keeping this secret for twenty-five years, I have decided to share it with you, my dear friend. I trust that you will keep an open mind and will read it with compassion. You will be surely blessed and amazed once you have gained this incredible knowledge for yourself.

My sincere wishes,

JR

CHAPTER 1

The Secret's Out

May 2027

Suzy was enjoying some peaceful quality time sitting on a bench on the cliffs of Capel-le-Ferne, one of her favourite places, looking out at the calm blue sea. Six sailing boats in the bay caught the cool breeze in their sails and bustled along together, racing back to the marina at Dover at the end of a fun day. The sun hung slightly to Suzy's right and was already making plans to set, casting a glittering pathway of golden rays across the sea.

She smiled contentedly and then thought about why she was here on this beautiful sunny Saturday afternoon.

Her beloved nan turned eighty years old today, and a family celebration had been planned for that evening, the sort of gathering of aunties, uncles, and cousins that usually only happened at weddings, funerals, and christenings, and Suzy really hoped it would be wonderful for Nan. Suzy hadn't seen most of the guests for years. But she groaned as she remembered the last family get-together that she attended. Uncle Bert always said the same tactless things every time Suzy met him.

At Grandad's birthday three years before, he had said, 'Suzy! It is Suzy, isn't it? Little Suzy look at you! I haven't seen you for years. Why, the last time I saw you, you were seeing that scrawny boyfriend with the broken nose and the silly grin, and those teeth!' He laughed. In a rather mocking manner, 'I wonder whatever happened to him.'

'He got his nose mended and his teeth fixed, and he grew up to be a very handsome man. My best friend married him, and we all adore him!'

Uncle Bert looked into Suzy's angry eyes and shuffled uncomfortably. 'Err, hum, yes, well . . . that's nice, dear. I see your Auntie Millie is here. Must go and say hello. We'll chat again later, hmm?' Red-faced, he scurried away

'Not if I can help it!' Suzy mumbled, as she left the room in disgust.

She had to admit, though, that on the whole, her family were darn good fun and smashing company. Uncle Bert was the exception. But she had escaped for a couple of hours to take in some fresh air, up on the cliffs, relax, and have a quick look down at the warren. Suzy planned to stay with Nan for a week or maybe two, so there would be plenty of time to visit with family, and see the warren properly, later.

From her bench on the cliff she could see across the bay and out to sea. There was France just standing on the horizon. The weather was so clear today that she could even make out the sand dunes. To her right, in the distance, were the little square bumps of Dungeness, and to her left, not so far down the coastline, were the big ferries rushing to and fro between Dover and various French ports. Huge jetfoil ships had replaced the ships that Susan had taken as a young girl, and they no longer pumped out that awful black smoke from their funnels since solar power had been introduced. She shook her head and smiled as she thought of all the controversy over them just twenty years before. No one could believe that it would be possible to run big engines with solar power, but it had happened. One more environmental issue solved.

She looked further to her right along the cliff edge and saw the café. Twenty-five years before it was The Cliff top Café and had plastic tables and chairs. It had since been rebuilt farther from the cliff edge for safety and to allow for more room for the magnificent paved veranda that looked out over the bay. It was now very modern, with stainless-steel tables and chairs that were graffiti and seagull poo proof. Suzy had to smile to herself as she remembered that dear little café from long ago with its pretty umbrellas (which were up on days when it wasn't too windy). It was enchanting in those days. Under the new management, the café was now smart, state of the art, and very busy.

Suzy looked down and down to her beautiful warren three hundred feet below. From this height, the tops of a forest of trees looked like a carpet of bushes. It was hard to believe that with all the changes in the world, this tiny spot had remained the same for the last twenty-five years.

The warren, a protected area of natural beauty, is a beautiful place to visit, as it is home to woodland creatures and birds of many different species. For ordinary human beings, the only way to get down there is to take the steps that have been hewn out of the cliff side and made with perfectly crafted driftwood.

It takes about fifteen minutes to reach the woods at the bottom of the steps. There, nestled in the warmth of the cliff and sheltered by the treetops, is the home of an array of the most beautiful ferns, which give the ground a tropical appearance.

Suzy always felt a wonderful sense of peace there as the sunrays shone through the trees. The only sounds she could hear were the rustling of leaves, the patter of little feet as rabbits and all sorts of other small creatures scurried away, birdsong, and the distant sound of the sea, harmonising to create a dreamlike atmosphere.

This was an enchanted, mysterious place, a tiny part of Capel-le-Ferne that many had tried to explore. The zigzag pathway and steps leading down from the café allowed people with the puff and stamina access down the cliff side, through the warren, over the railway bridge, and onto the beach, but the woodlands and grounds around the footpaths were now out of bounds to sightseers. Visitors often commented on the sounds and movements around them as they descended the cliff side and wandered along the winding pathway through the warren and carefully walked along the public footpath.

There had been many reports over the past twenty years of bleating animal sounds that visitors suspected were sheep or possibly goats, and other visitors saw bright fluorescent lights and the bushes parting as if something which couldn't be seen was walking through them. Some had reported a very strange feeling as if something had rushed passed them, creating a whoosh of air in its wake.

Had it been a large bird? Or rabbits running through the bushes, maybe?

No one had ever seen anything tangible that would explain these happenings, or, at least, no one had come forward with an explanation. Most reports had been dismissed as being caused by sea breezes, sea mist or low clouds, loose rocks falling.

Suzy smiled to herself when she remembered the news flash on the local TV station ten years ago:

UFO Spotted in the Warren

A woman walking her dog reported to the police that she had seen a glowing object floating high up above the warren. Sergeant Boswell at police headquarters said that he didn't believe there was any cause for concern. There are many logical explanations for such reflections by the sea.

It was explained a week later on the local news, as light reflecting off the chairlifts. Suzy remembered breathing a huge sigh of relief after that particular scare. It wasn't always easy to keep her secret.

The warren now belonged to her. Well, the special part, anyway a four-mile area from cliff top to the railway line that formed a giant oval on the map. She had bought it with the paxtey gold she had been given as a reward from one of her adventures, so that all her little friends could be protected.

The railway owned adjacent land that ran through the warren to the beach, and she had agreed with the local authority when they built a chairlift over the warren for beach visitors who couldn't manage the walk down the zigzag path. The cable car looked really impressive, with each cabin like a brightly coloured spaceship with just enough room for two. They only operated in good weather and in the holiday season from May to September.

Suzy had insisted that a special fence be built at either side of the footpath so that visitors didn't stray into her woods and marshland, and along it, she had erected a sign that said:

BEWARE OF ROCK FALLS
AND QUICKSAND
FOR YOUR SAFETY,
STAY ON FOOTPATHS PROVIDED
HAVE A NICE DAY

Sometimes overly curious people would ignore the notice and try to climb over the fence, but as soon as they planted their hands on the fence's wires and lifted their feet from the ground, they'd see a flash of luminous rainbow colours, and their curiosity would disappear, and they would climb down and carry on their jolly way as if nothing had happened. Suzy knew that rock falls were very rare and that there was no quicksand here, but that sign, and the fence, were the only safe ways to protect her friends. Had it really happened twenty-five years ago this month when she met all those wonderful friends down there in the warren? There had been a full moon that day, too.

She stared out to sea once more. Her hair, just as fair as it had been then, although now shoulder length, caught the sea breeze across the cliffs. A smile came to her lips and a happy glow to her eyes as she remembered those precious friends, the deep blue sea and the deep blue sky became a big movie screen onto which she projected her memories.

'It seems so long ago now. I was just twelve years old,' she whispered quietly to herself. 'And yet I can remember it as if it were yesterday.'

May 2002

It all started in Nan's attic.

Have you ever been exploring in an old attic or barn, where, in every corner you look, you find interesting lumps of fluff and dust, neatly woven webs so thick and chunky they look like grey candyfloss with enormous spiders sitting in them, the sort that have lived there so long they think they own the place? That's what Nan's attic was like on the day she found her friend Scratch. Whenever she stayed at Nan's house and it rained too heavily to go out, she always felt drawn to the attic, even though there were big spiders around. Poor Suzy was terrified of spiders but as long as they kept away from her she could pretend they weren't there.

She jiggled and wriggled up the attic stairs, shaking her shoulders to the S Club 7 CD playing in Nan's music centre.

'Don't stop moving to the S Club beat! Dada do dee dada dum dum *da*!' she sang at the top of her voice to her favourite group, waving her hands and arms as they did in the video.

'I hope she's not thinking of earning a living with that voice!' Grandad shouted.

'Stop being mean,' Nan responded.

Suzy stood at the top of the stairs and looked around. She felt the excitement of finding something new, as she did every time she went up there, but she didn't yet know what it was that she was supposed to find.

She had been having the same strange dream for the past year since her eleventh birthday: She frantically searched through boxes, drawers, and cupboards for something, or someone, that she knew she was supposed to find. Then, just as she smiled and said hello to what it was she was looking for, she woke up. It was so aggravating. She hoped one day she would stay asleep long enough to see what she was supposed to find, but in the meantime, she planned to explore the attic every chance she got while awake.

Big boxes, wooden boxes, cardboard boxes, a chest of drawers, old tea chests—stuff was everywhere? Suzy sat on a stool and picked up a cardboard box full of photographs. She loved looking at photos, especially the really old black-and-white ones. Some of them were so funny. Sure enough, she found the one of her great-grandma Pearl as a little girl. She was sitting on a beach somewhere in England, wearing a striped swimsuit with sleeves and legs covered and a huge bow on the side of her head. In the front was her mother, Suzy's great-great-grandmother, fully clothed and wearing a hat with a big brim and all the ladies standing beside Pearl wore hats like flowerpots and were fully clothed, except for their feet and ankles, as they paddled in the shallow water.

What strange clothes they wore all those years ago, Suzy thought, smiling with amazement. *They must have been so hot wearing so much clothing on the beach.*

She turned the photo over and found July 1920-something written there; she couldn't make out the exact year.

'Coo! That's yonks' ago!'

Suzy carried on flicking through photos for a while, and then, sighing, she put them all back in the box and looked around for something else to search.

In the corner on the chest of drawers was an old wind-up record player with a label that read 'His Master's Voice Gramophone Player' and featured a picture of a dear little dog looking down a strange trumpet thing.

She decided to play a record that was one of Nan's all-time favourites, 'Jailhouse Rock' by Elvis Presley. She also decided to dress up for the occasion.

'Now where's that cancan petticoat I found the other day with all those smashing colours?' she whispered to herself. *Ah! Found it.* It was a bit dusty, but Suzy didn't mind.

Once she had the skirt on, Suzy put a huge plastic record on the turntable, wound the gramophone's handle furiously to start the record moving round and round, and then lifted the massive metal arm (well, it seemed massive) the round head with the needle in it filled her hand. She moved it across and into a groove on the spinning record.

'Going to a party at the county jail!' Not a bad sound for such an old contraption. Suzy twirled and rocked to the music.

Nan heard the record playing and popped upstairs to see what Suzy was up to. There she was, swishing her skirt round, stirring up dust, and disturbing the spiders. Nan chuckled quietly. *What a sight! I wish I had my camera handy,* she thought.

Suzy looked up to see Nan watching her and really went into superstar mode, spinning so that the skirt whizzed out even further, waving her arms to and fro She held out her right arm so gracefully, wriggling her hips to the beat, and saw, sitting on her hand, the biggest spider she had ever seen.

Suzy's smile became a look of horror, and a piercing scream burst forth from her throat. Her heart lurched up to two hundred beats a minute; her arm became a lasso twirling above her head and launching the spider into orbit across the attic.

She squealed and screamed and jumped up and down hysterically until the petticoat fell to the floor, and she ran over to Nan, who was laughing so hard that tears were rolling down her cheeks.

'It's not funny!' Suzy squealed. 'Stop laughing! I was nearly eaten alive by a giant spider, and all you can do is laugh.' She ran down the stairs. 'I'm never going up there again!'

Nan turned off the record player and looked over at the spider as it skulked off under a cupboard.

'I don't suppose the spider enjoyed his ride much either.'

She laughed again and followed Suzy downstairs.

One day she'll discover him. Any day now, I think. She went into the kitchen and put the kettle on for a nice cup of tea and thought a chocolate biscuit or two to have with our tea would be perfect and calming for someone terrified of spiders.

Chapter 2

Meet Scratch

Not long after the great spider incident, on a miserable rainy day, Suzy couldn't go outdoors, and she had already listened to music, read her books, and even done homework that didn't have to be in for weeks. She came out of her room and looked at the steps leading up to the attic. Those steps were like a magnet drawing her towards them. With a couple of deep breaths, she plucked up her courage and slowly went up to the attic.

Which box shall I open and explore today? She wondered.

She looked all around to make sure there weren't any spiders near her, and just at that moment, the sun shone through the attic's two windows.

Hmm. Perhaps I can go outdoors after all, Suzy thought.

Suddenly, out of the corner of her eye, Suzy saw something move in a corner between the ceiling and the wall.

'What was that?'

She stood very still and peered into the corner but couldn't see anything very clearly from where she was standing, so she found a large wooden box sturdy enough to stand on and pushed it across the floor.

'Ooh, I do hope it's not one of those blooming great spiders again,' Suzy mumbled. 'I'll die of fright; I know I will.'

As she pushed the box, she looked again and definitely saw a dark something in that corner, but she couldn't tell what it was, and now it wasn't moving.

All thoughts of going outdoors had left Suzy's mind by the time she finally reached the corner, puffing and blowing from the weight of the big box; her mind was totally absorbed by this dark something. There was still no movement. Perhaps it had seen her coming.

She climbed onto the box and got as close to the dark blob as possible. As her eyes focused and the blob became clearer, she realised to her astonishment that it was a huge chrysalis. She jumped off the box and wondered whether she should call Nan.

No, Nan's having forty winks, and I don't want to disturb her. And anyway, it might be nothing to worry about, Suzy decided. She got back on the box for another look. The chrysalis was at least fourteen inches tall and six inches wide, with one end fixed to the ceiling. It hung above a clean shelf with a soft, clean cushion on it.

How is it possible that the whole attic is dusty and grubby except for this shelf? Suzy wondered. *This is very strange. And just look at the size of it! I have never seen a chrysalis so huge.*

Just then, the chrysalis wriggled, making Suzy jump and fall off the box. She gasped for breath and was decidedly nervous now. Suppose this turned out to be a dangerous creature, something poisonous, even!

The sunrays then shone on it, reflecting a rainbow of colours that was softly radiating across the chrysalis as it wriggled. Suzy peered more closely at its top and gasped again. She was sure a glowing face peered back at her, and the chrysalis wriggled frantically now. This really scared her, and she jumped down and ran to the top of the stairs.

"Nan!" Suzy screamed at the top of her voice. 'Come and see what I've found, *quickly*!"

'I'm on my way,' Nan groaned, trying to sound awake.

Nan came up the stairs as quickly as she could with her dodgy knees.

'Whatever's wrong?' she said.

Suzy ran back to the box. 'Quick, look at this!'

An opening appeared along the side of the chrysalis, and it grew wider and wider, revealing something fleshy covered by a translucent, brightly coloured wing.

'It must be some kind of giant butterfly or moth,' Suzy said.

Nan walked over to the shelf. 'So, you've discovered him, then.'

'I don't understand. What do you mean *him*?'

'Suzy, you are about to see something and meet a being so rare that you must promise me right now that you will keep this our secret. You must *never* tell anyone about it, ever. Promise me, Suzy, before he comes out.'

Suzy looked at Nan with astonishment but realised that now was not the time for questions. She quickly replied, 'I promise, Nan. I promise it will be our secret forever.' She hugged Nan, and they both turned back to the shelf to watch what the chrysalis was doing. 'Did you know this was here?' Suzy whispered.

'Yes. Every other year at about this time, I clean the shelf and put the cushion there so that he has something soft and clean to fall on,' Nan whispered.

'Is it a giant butterfly?'

'No. Just wait and see. I promise, I'll answer all your questions later. Please don't be scared.'

But Suzy didn't feel scared at all anymore. In fact, she was excited, as if she were about to see something she had been waiting for all her life.

There was one more wriggle, and out the 'something' slid with a soft, wet plop onto the cushion. It lay still for a while, and then the sun, which had gone behind a cloud, came out again and shone right on the cushion, highlighting the wings still wrapped around the creature's body. As it dried in the sun and the wings unfurled, the most astonishing thing happened, tiny feet and then legs appeared, and then hands and arms, and then the creature stood. It was a small, perfect person.

'Suzy, meet Scratch, Nan said proudly.

'Oh, Nan! Isn't it beautiful?' Suzy breathlessly whispered.

'Yes, I've always thought that this moment is beautiful.'

'You mean you've seen it before?' Suzy said, still whispering.

'Yes. For six years now, Scratch has chosen to hibernate in our house.'

'Six years! And you never told me?'

'Well, you were too young to understand, and I realised that you would meet him when the time was right, which, as it turns out, is now.'

'Oh, there is so much to know. What is he, a fairy? or an elf?

'I am a paxtey,' whispered a tiny, gentle voice.

Suzy stared at him open-mouthed and almost fell off the box, as her knees went wobbly.

'There you are, Suzy. You can talk to him yourself now. He's ready.' Nan smiled.

Suzy was struck dumb as Scratch folded his wings neatly down his back and simply stood there, his body covered in a suit that reminded her of a cat suit made of a material that she couldn't describe, as it wasn't human, but that could have been made from his wings, and on his feet were boots of a beige material like a very fine chamois leather fastened with the tiniest of mother-of-pearl buttons. He looked about twelve to fourteen inches tall

'I'm dreaming. I'm going to wake up in a minute and realise this is all a dream. Suzy pinched herself and then, for good measure, slapped her face. 'Ouch! I'm not dreaming.' She took a deep breath and said in a shaky voice, 'What's a paxtey?'

Scratch smiled and said in a gentle voice, 'A paxtey, that's me. I'm not an elf or a fairy or a pixie. I am a small person like a pixie, and I have wings like a fairy, but that is where the likenesses end.' His voice sounded like a normal boy's, but it seemed to be coming from far away because he was so small.

'Are there many more of you?' Suzy asked, trying to regain her composure.

'There are many of us all over the world.'

'I don't understand. If there are so many of you, how is it that I've never seen any of you? And how is it that I've never heard anyone talk about paxteys?"

'Only special humans ever get to see us. You see, we can fly so fast that it looks as if we have vanished, and we are able to see farther than any other living creature as well. Do you see these fine hairs on the tips of my ears?'

'Yes,' Suzy whispered.

'They enable me to hear sounds from great distances.'

'Wow!'

'So, you see, we paxteys can quite easily keep away from anyone that we do not wish to see us.'

'Who gave you the name of Scratch?' is that your real name?

'Many years ago when Nan discovered me, I hadn't yet been given a proper name, and Nan said that I was a mere scratch of a thing because I was so small, and then she decided that that was what she was going to call me. I have proudly carried the name ever since.'

'There's so much I don't understand, so much I need to know,' Suzy groaned, utterly overwhelmed.

'Perhaps you might save your questions till later, because I have to think about the paxtey haven now.'

'What's a paxtey haven?' Suzy asked.

'It's a meeting of all the paxteys at the first full moon after we come out of hibernation, and tonight happens to be the full moon.'

'Where do you have to go for this meeting? Would I be allowed to come?'

'It's held in the warren, and yes, you may come, for you have seen me today, which means you have been chosen as a special companion. We will no doubt find out the reason you were chosen while we are there.'

The warren? Suzy thought. *That old place? Nothing ever happens down there. Why on earth would someone so special want to go down there?*

'At the very least, the haven will answer many of your questions.' Scratch smiled as he settled down on his cushion for a rest.

Suzy left him then to sleep and fully recover and went back downstairs to Nan to have her tea. Never mind Scratch, Suzy needed time to recover and take this all in as well! She sat at the kitchen table bursting with excitement as she sipped her mug of tea. Nan and Grandad smiled happily, and Nan said she was so relieved that Suzy had taken it so well. Nan explained that she and Grandad were just sleep carers for paxteys but Scratch was special because he had become a beloved friend to them both during the time he had spent with them. After tea, Nan suggested that Suzy go off to bed and have a rest before she started out on her adventure.

Adventure? Suzy wondered. *Why is Nan calling it an* adventure? *I'm only going to some kind of special gathering, not going on an adventure!* 'Hmm, strange,' she mumbled.

She settled down on her bed and went straight off to sleep thanks to all the excitement of that afternoon.

Suzy had her usual dream: There she was, searching boxes, searching drawers, searching tea chests, spiders all around her, and then, there he was in that beautiful light.

'Hello, Suzy.' His little face came into the light. 'My name is Scratch.'

'At long last my search is over,' Suzy whispered. Little did she know it was just the beginning?

Chapter 3

The Paxtey Haven

Quite late that night, when the moon was shining brightly, Suzy heard someone calling her.

'Who's that?' she mumbled, still half asleep. She was cosy and warm and happy to stay where she was.

'Suzy! Suzy!' It was Scratch calling. Suzy opened her eyes and looked toward the light of the moon shining through her window and saw him hovering outside her window.

Nan must have heard him calling, too, because she walked into Suzy's bedroom at the same time, talking rather loudly, Suzy thought. On went the light.

'Time to wake up, Suzy quickly now. Scratch is waiting, and you've got to get washed and dressed yet. Put on a warm coat and hat, and here's your scarf. It's a damp, chilly night, but you can take it off when you get there.'

Suzy jumped out of bed, tripped over her shoes, and fell backwards on the bed, knocking over the bedside lamp.

"Oh, what on earth is going on? What's the time? It feels like the middle of the night.' Suzy looked at the clock, which read 11.30. At night!

'Nan, are you mad? It's the middle of the night!'

'Yes, it certainly is,' Nan said, 'and normally nothing on earth would move me to let you go out at such a time, but this is different.

Suzy rushed around gathering her clothes 'Where's those pink socks? I'm going to wear my pink jeans and cream jumper' Nan continued talking.

'Listen to Scratch and follow every instruction he gives you. Just for once, Suzy, keep this closed.' She tapped Suzy's lips. 'Watch and listen.'

'Nan, you sound like someone off the telly!' Suzy laughed as she ran out of the house to find her friend.

Nan shook her head and called, 'Enjoy yourself'

As soon as Suzy stepped outside into the dark night, Scratch appeared in front of her face. She jumped.

'You gave me such a fright!'

'Hello, Suzy. I'm so glad you're coming. Follow me.' He and Suzy waved to Nan and disappeared into the night, quickly and quietly leaving

Nan's garden and turning right into the lane. At the end of the lane, keeping close to the hedgerow, they turned right again, and Suzy walked on for another ten minutes, with Scratch flying in front of her. In the quiet of the night, Suzy could vaguely hear the faint hum of his wings.

"You're not nervous, are you?' Scratch called.

"Just a little," Suzy replied.

Scratch stopped and flew back to her side and said in a calm, gentle voice, "I promise you that tonight will be wonderful for you. I will stay with you, and you'll be fine."

"Thank you." Suzy sighed.

It was a beautiful night millions of stars and a huge moon hung in the clear sky. Suzy's thoughts went to the warren. *It'll be pitch dark, cold and damp, and muddy down there. Nan never said anything about a torch, and I've got to get down all those old steps. Good thing there's a full moon because that's all the light there'll be.* Normally she would never be allowed out after dark, let alone this late at night.

Scratch stopped and pointed to the left. 'We're going to go down there.'

Suzy was at the edge of the cliff a couple of metres away from where the usual steps were.

I suppose he is expecting me to climb down there, but they say it's about three hundred feet to the bottom!

When she came up to Scratch, she saw a misty patch at the cliff's edge which, on closer inspection, turned out to be a glowing golden gate. Suzy pushed it, and it gently opened. As she walked through, a flight of stairs appeared as if it were floating in the clouds.

How beautiful! She thought as Scratch flew ahead of her down the steps.

'Come on! It's perfectly safe, I know it's a long way down but these stairs will make it much easier than those old ones'

That's reassuring, Suzy thought. The gate closed behind her and disappeared.

A man came strolling along with his dog a few minutes later. He didn't know anything about the splendid golden gate as he looked across the cliffs and out to sea, admiring the lights as they flickered and danced on the fishing boats and the glorious moonlight as it glittered across the sea like silver fairy dust on the dark water. He also didn't know what was about to unfold in the warren three hundred feet below him, but his dog knew. The dog barked like mad at the spot where Suzy had gone through the gate and wagged his tail as if he had seen an old friend. He really wanted to go down that lovely golden staircase, but the gate was shut. Besides, he had to stay with his master.

'Sparky, stop that noise! Come over here and leave the rabbits alone.'

To keep up with Scratch, Suzy ran quickly down the steps which seemed to be part of the cliff yet somehow also floating in twinkling clouds. They zigzagged down the cliff face. Further down she heard singing and laughing.

Finally, Suzy stepped onto the floor of the warren, and the sight that unfolded before her was beyond anything she could have imagined: in every direction were the most unusual and exquisite things to see, animals, and tiny people like Scratch. Her feet were frozen to the spot at the bottom of those stairs as she took in the scenery.

In a patch of clear ground lit by the moonlight sat six paxteys—two played pipes, two played banjos and one played a triangle that stood on the ground taller than his body strung with hundreds of tiny bells which, on closer inspection, Suzy discovered were actually made from cockleshells. As for the other little chap, well, Suzy couldn't help giggling. When Scratch had mentioned other paxteys, she hadn't imagined that one would be wearing fashionable dreadlocks, but sure enough, there he was. And his dreadlocks were coloured in luminous green and yellow! He played a kit of six drums all made from blue-crab shells.

Animals sat together in small groups watching and enjoying the music. Hundreds of birds were chattering away in the tree branches. There was no fear or nervousness among any of the animals.

The most incredible part of all this was seeing animals that would normally be enemies sitting together. Foxes sat with rabbits, rats and mice sat together under the perches of owls. Seagulls sat with crows, pigeons sat with the sparrows and finches and even the sparrow hawk! To Suzy's left and halfway up a tree she could just make out a jay sitting and talking with a blackbird!

Suzy looked at the pond in a corner of the clearing and gasped when she saw, their heads clearly visible at the surface, a catfish, a perch, and a couple of sticklebacks all side by side. Above them gnats and dragonflies buzzed, and the fish made no attempt to eat each other, let alone the insects.

For this one night, they would be peaceful as they enjoyed the paxtey haven. A group of paxteys sat together laughing and chanting:

Hey, hey, hey, cheery day!

Hi, hi, hi, happy night!

Welcome you are,

All those from afar,

To join the paxtey haven!

Hey, hey, hey, Mr Owl,

Sitting there with gentle Pea Fowl;

Hi, hi, hi, Mr Rat,

Sitting there with Mr Cat,

Welcome you are

To join us this night

At the famous paxtey haven!

Most paxteys joined in singing. Suzy remained at the bottom of the stairs, still marvelling at the incredible picture. Scratch rushed around greeting all the other paxteys and the animals, many of which he appeared to know very well, as he hugged the fox and kissed the rabbits and all those cats with long legs.

Cats? They're not cats, Suzy thought. *That's incredible! They're miniature goats! And their kids are the size of the smallest kittens*

'Oh my word. I can't believe this. There are so many strange things to see.' Suzy had a very strong feeling that this was only the beginning of the strangeness.

In the middle of this gathering was what appeared to be the oldest paxtey of them all? He sat on a large chalk stone, which seemed very comfy with a cushion of moss. He was smoking a long white pipe and was really impressive to look at with white curly hair stretching down his back and a thin, white goatee reaching to his knees. There was a large group of Paxtey's sat on the ground around him with a look of reverence on their faces.

Suzy was so busy staring at the scene that she hadn't realised Scratch had returned and was standing on a low branch beside her.

'That's old Chamali,' he said proudly, 'which in the ancient paxtey language means *storyteller*. All the young ones are waiting for Chamali to tell them a tale of the old days.'

Suzy turned to Scratch with a smile and a look of wonder on her face.

'Some say he is at least a hundred and fifty years old, but no one knows for sure. I don't think he even knows himself.' Scratch laughed. 'Let me take you round to meet everyone.'

'Oh, no, Scratch, I couldn't,' Suzy exclaimed. 'I won't know what to say!'

'Just say hello, silly Suzy.' With a smile, Scratch gently nudged her forwards.

Just at that moment, the singing started anew:

> Hey, hey, hey, here they are,
> Two friends, Scratch and Suzy.
> Hi, hi, hi, from the Capel Ridge,
> They join us fresh and oozy!

'Oozy?' Suzy puzzled. 'What's that supposed to mean?'

The paxtey in the dreadlocks laughed and shrugged.

'I think it was the best they could do on the spur of the moment.' Scratch chuckled. 'Now, let me introduce you. Over there playing the flutes are Toomy and Tooby, that's Purly on the triangle, Twee and Twig playing the paxtey banjos, and that's Jam on the drums.'

'Hello, Suzy! Welcome to the paxtey haven!' they called out in unison.

Suzy shyly waved and smiled and said, 'Thank you very much.'

Very carefully (Suzy didn't want to tread on anyone), she moved around the groups of paxteys and weaved in and out among all the happy creatures.

'Scratch this has to be the most wonderful moment in the whole of my life. I feel so privileged to see this. Am I allowed to ask questions now?'

'Of course,' Scratch said with a nod

'I just wondered about the goats. How did they come to be so tiny? Are they magical like paxteys?'

'Perhaps I may be able to answer that question for you.'

Suzy spun round and realised that there standing in front of her was Chamali the storyteller.

She gasped. 'Hello sir I'm very pleased to meet you.'

'Likewise, I'm sure. Someone find Suzy a seat.' Chamali waved his hand in the air.

Within seconds, a seat made of woven twigs and leaves came floating down from a tree carried by two large seagulls. Suzy found it squishy and comfortable, as though it had been moulded to her shape. She relaxed into the chair, tucking her feet under her to keep from kicking any of the very little creatures. All went quiet as Chamali spoke.

'You asked about the goats, so I have decided to tell the story of the goat family tonight.'

Suzy smiled, and the young ones squealed with delight as everyone sat comfortably and relaxed, readying themselves for the tale.

'In the early 1950s, several goats escaped from an abattoir near here. They hid in the warren and decided to stay, as it was the ideal home for them because here, they had hills and dales to run up and down and play in and keep watch for predators, and they had all the vegetation they could eat.'

As Suzy listened to Chamali, a mist appeared in from of him and cleared in the middle to reveal an image of goats running through the warren like a movie. She was now watching the tale unfold before her very eyes.

'Magic,' she whispered to herself.

'The young goats were very happy, and soon their families grew in great numbers. For a long time, they lived very happily with all the animals of the warren, and there was never any reason to doubt that life would continue like this forever.

'One sunny morning, the rabbits and the foxes and all the creatures of the warren were woken by the seagulls, who shrieked a warning: "Beware, beware! Man comes!"

'The sun disappeared behind a cloud, and a terrible silence fell over the warren. Then, heavy footsteps echoed through the trees, getting louder and louder! Everybody hid, except the goats. They were so happy that they didn't think they had anything to fear.

'Bang! Bang! Bang! Shots rang out.

'The terrible screams of the goats were too much to bear for the other creatures of the warren. All they could do was cry in despair for their friends from their hiding places. For three days, they endured the terror of the men coming back and forth to the warren. They believed that soon it would be their turn to suffer the goats' fate and that happiness would never again return to the warren.

'By the end of the third day, all the goats were gone except one family. A Nanny goat, a Billy goat, and their two daughters and a nephew who had lost his parents had found a small cave, and they huddled together there knowing that soon it would be their turn. But then, a paxtey called Skeet found them.

'"Thank goodness I've found you! I've been looking everywhere for you," Skeet said.

'When the other goats saw Skeet, they all wailed at the same time, 'What are we to do? Where can we go?'

'Shush, shush. I have an idea. Follow me quickly.' Skeet led the family further into the warren, where he knew of another, deeper cave.

'In you go now,' Skeet said. 'Whatever you hear or see, don't come out. Wait there until I come back for you.'

'Flying at his greatest speed, Skeet gathered bushes and blocked the cave entrance, making it look as if the vegetation had always been there, and then he disappeared. There were a few more bleats and a few more gunshots, and all went quiet.

'That's the lot,' one man shouted.

'Righto,' another responded. 'Gather 'em up and let's get out of here.'

'The goat family stayed huddled together as the footsteps of the men gradually disappeared into the distance, replaced by an unbelievable silence over the warren. Not even the cheep of a bird could be heard. The goat family waited . . .

'Until the bushes at the entrance to the cave were pulled away, and they all shrieked from fear, but then they saw Skeet who had bought more paxteys with him.

'The hunters have gone at last, they seem to think they've finished their terrible deed and have killed all the goats.'

'The goat family breathed a huge sigh of relief and started to walk out of the cave, but Skeet stopped them.

'Just a moment my friends are here', Skeet nodded to the other paxteys, 'I have had a meeting, and we have decided that there is only one way you will be able to stay safe in the warren. You must never be seen by human eyes again, and to do that, you must be able to hide in caves smaller than this one."

The ten paxteys, including Skeet, flew in circles around the goats faster and faster until they blurred into a giant, luminous, rainbow circle. The colours grew brighter, surrounding each goat with his or her own luminous aura, and the goats shrank until the adults were the size of small cats and the kids were the size of tiny kittens. Finally, Skeet and his friends reappeared.

"From now on," Skeet said, "you will only be seen by the other creatures of the warren, and these auras will enable all paxteys to know where you are so that they can protect you."

Chamali paused and looked slowly around smiling at the many tear-stained faces.

'The goat family had survived that terrible time, and after that, with the protection of the paxteys, they flourished.' He clapped his hands, and out of the bushes appeared dozens of tiny goats encircled in sparkling colours. Everyone cheered, clapped, and hugged the goats, and as the goats joined the others, the paxtey band sang.

Hey, hey, hey, wondrous day,

The little goats are here to stay!

Suzy cheered and clapped, and with her eyes full of tears, she turned to Scratch.

'Aren't they just lovely in all those colours? There are so many goats! They all look so happy. This is just brilliant Scratch, it really is!'

Scratch cheered along with everyone, too, with each creature celebrating in its own way, soaking up the happy atmosphere.

Everyone had just finished cheering and resumed chatting among themselves, when they heard a shrill 'Kaa! Kaa!' coming from a giant bird, he had launched himself from the branch of the tallest tree above the warren and allowed his fourteen-foot wingspan to glide gently down to the clearing.

Suzy was so startled she fell off her chair, just missing a goat and sending a group of young paxteys off screaming.

Apart from causing a terrible draught, the bird landed very gently considering his size. This was definitely the biggest bird Suzy had ever seen.

'Welcome, Bira. This is indeed a surprise," Chamali said. 'And what business could the King's messenger have with us this night? Have you come to join our happy gathering?'

Bira gently waddled across to Chamali and appeared to start a conversation, but try as she might, Suzy couldn't hear what they said. Suzy got up, brushed herself down, and sat back in her seat.

'Have you ever seen a bird like that before?' she quietly whispered to Scratch as she settled in.

'No,' Scratch responded in a whisper, 'but I have heard of them. He is an albatross, and they don't usually come to this part of the world unless on very important business from the King.'

Everyone sat quietly waiting, and the young paxteys returned to their seats to watch, wide-eyed and curious.

After a few minutes that seemed like hours, Chamali cleared his throat. 'Gather around, everyone. I have very important news.'

Everyone moved in as close as they could.

'Tomorrow, we will have to meet once again here in the warren, as we are going to have a visit from the Great King himself, for he has a matter of grave importance to tell us about. We will all meet here tomorrow just as we have this night when the moon is at its highest to honour the Great King and to listen to him. We will not have a celebration but a deliberation. Until then, we should all go back to our dwellings to rest.'

All the creatures, including the paxteys, quietly left the clearing, and just as Suzy headed for the stairs, Scratch called to her, 'No, Suzy, you don't have to go back up those stairs alone.' He and four of his paxtey friends carried her chair to her at the foot of the stairs, and Suzy sat just as Scratch and friends lifted it up the cliff.

Suzy giggled. This was such fun! 'Look everyone, I'm flying!' she called out as she waved to all her new friends on the ground. She watched

Bira the albatross take off out to sea, his huge shape silhouetted in the moonlight, and she stopped giggling.

In a few minutes, she was back on the clifftop and walking home with Scratch. They remained quiet, absorbed in their thoughts about tomorrow.

When Suzy went inside, she found Nan dozing in the armchair waiting for her return. Suzy gently kissed her on the cheek. 'I'm home, Nan.'

Nan opened her eyes. 'Have you had a nice time, love?'

'Oh, Nan, it was the most brilliant, fantastic time, but I'm so tired.'

'Then let's go to bed. We can talk it all over tomorrow.' Nan said with a smile.

Suzy made herself a cup of drinking chocolate and then followed Nan up stairs.

'Goodnight, love,' Nan said.

'Night, Nan.' Suzy blew her a kiss and disappeared into her bedroom.

She fell on her bed and with a deep sigh and thought about tomorrow night. *Chamali said there would be a deliberation, which must be pretty serious. It felt like a warning when he said it. I wonder what'll happen. I'll not think about that for now and just remember all the lovely things I've seen and heard tonight.*

Suzy finished her lovely cup of hot chocolate, snuggled down under the duvet, and went to sleep with a very contented smile on her face.

Chapter 4

His Royal Highness King Tobias III

The next morning Suzy awoke to the sun shining on her face through the window. As she yawned, the sweet smell of toast and bacon caught her nose, and she realised, 'I'm starving!'

She jumped out of bed and grabbed her dressing gown. But then the memory of last night popped back into her mind, and she flopped back down on her bed, gasping in disbelief.

'Was that not just the greatest time of my life? All those little people, Chamali the storyteller, the music, those goats!' she whispered to herself. 'But what is going to happen tonight?'

A moment later, she got up again and ran downstairs, calling, 'Hello, Nan, hello, Grandad!'

Suzy stopped in her tracks when she reached the kitchen doorway, her slippers skidding on the polished floor. Sitting on the table was Scratch—on his own little pine chair at his own little pine table placed *on* the table opposite Nan—eating his breakfast. Grandad sat at the head of the table, and Nan sat to his right.

Suzy joined them, grinning from ear to ear. 'Scratch, you're here too?'

'Of course I try to be here every morning if I can 'He replied.

'This is great!' Suzy said between bites of toast.

'I haven't thought about it before, but what do paxteys eat, Scratch?' She looked over to examine what Scratch had on his plate and found fruit and berries.

'We eat many things. Fruit, wild berries, nuts, herbs, some wild flowers, even some wild grasses.'

Suzy was impressed that Scratch was a healthy eater but preferred to tuck in to her bacon and eggs. As they ate, she and Scratch told Nan and Grandad all about the paxtey haven, and Nan and Grandad were amazed at the thought that all the different animals got along so well together. They chuckled when Suzy told them about the band and Jam's dreadlocks, and luminous colours and they were very impressed with Chamali's story and so sad to hear about the goats. Although Nan and Grandad said that they had met Chamali, they had never had the pleasure of listening to any of his stories.

'What on earth do you think might bring the Great King out here?' Nan said.

'It has to be something serious,' Grandad said. 'The Great King has never come to our warren before.'

'That's what the other paxteys were saying,' Scratch said. 'Some of them have seen him. but never has he been here.'

'I bet he's coming for some purpose that neither of you have thought about,' Nan said.

'What's that?' Suzy and Scratch chimed in together.

'Don't you think that it's too much of a coincidence that on the night of Suzy's introduction to the paxtey haven, suddenly, the Great King is coming? Perhaps Suzy has been chosen to help in some great mystery, whatever it might be.'

'Nan please!' Suzy squealed. 'What could the King want with me? I've got so much to learn yet. I wouldn't be of any help to anyone.'

'I don't know about that,' Nan said. 'We humans have our uses in the paxtey world. Don't underestimate your usefulness, Suzy. All I'm saying is you should be prepared.'

'What do you think, Scratch?' Suzy asked.

'Well, I think Nan could be on to something. My senses have been twitching since I woke up at first bird chorus, and that's always a warning. As Nan says, we will need to be prepared.'

Grandad nodded and smiled. 'If there's anything I can help you with, anything you want made, just let me know. I would be honoured to help.'

'Thanks, Grandad,' Suzy and Scratch said in unison. Suzy finished her tea, and Scratch finished his morning dew and blackberry juice.

'Suzy, for the time being, ordinary life goes on, and there's the washing up and shopping to do,' Nan reminded her.

So with her feet firmly back on the ground, Suzy got on with her chores and then got dressed and headed off to the shopping centre with Nan. Scratch stayed home to help Grandad in the garden.

At the shopping centre, Nan rigged Suzy out with clothes for every possible contingency: there were clothes for the heat, clothes for the cold, waterproof shoes, and shoes for comfort. They dashed in and out of all the stores, and Suzy thoroughly enjoyed herself.

As they were walking back to the car, she said, 'You know, it's really nice of you to buy me all these things, but don't you think the situation's a bit dodgy?'

'Dodgy? What do you mean?'

'Well, if you're wrong and the King doesn't need my help, you will have spent all that money for nothing.'

Nan smiled a knowing smile. 'I don't think this will have been for nothing; I really don't think so.'

They arrived home just in time for lunch. Nan put the kettle on and called to Grandad in the garden, 'we're home, dear! Coming in for lunch?'

'Won't be a moment,' Grandad called back.

Scratch then appeared in the doorway with a big grin on his face. 'Have you had a nice time?'

'Yes, but Nan insisted on buying me all these clothes in case I need them. Look.' Suzy pointed at all the shopping bags. 'She says she's got a feeling.'

'Don't question it,' Scratch said, still showing that funny grin. 'Nan's feelings are usually right, and you should be prepared.'

Grandad then appeared in the doorway behind Scratch with the smile he got when he had a surprise.

'I know that look,' Nan said. 'What have you two been up to?'

'Oh, we've just done a few jobs around the garden and repaired the summer house,' Grandad said.

'And not too soon, I've been waiting for the summer house to be repaired for years,' Nan said.

'There you are, then. I'll give it a lick of paint later and it will be as good as new, ready for the summer, if it ever comes.'

The rest of the day flew by quickly but quietly, as everyone relaxed and napped. Just as she had done the previous night, Suzy had a few hours' sleep before she and Scratch set off for the warren.

'Oh, dear, Scratch last night I was excited, but tonight I really have the collywobbles.'

'Same here,' Scratch replied. 'I'm really filled with curiosity. 'Do you think the King will want to speak to me? Should I even be there?' Suzy muttered.

'I know you are meant to be there, so don't worry. Let's just wait and see what happens, shall we?'

Scratch pointed to the golden gate and the stairs leading to the warren; they had been so busy chatting that Suzy hadn't noticed that they'd arrived. It was getting late, but, fortunately, she knew where to go this time, so she ran down the stairs as quickly as she could.

When she got to the bottom, she was amazed at how many more paxteys were there than the night before, and the newcomers were wearing slightly different clothing to the local Capel warren paxteys. Although the newcomers' clothes were made of the same wonderful, indescribable material, some wore waistcoats over shirts and separate leggings, and some also wore cloaks, rather than the one-piece suits the locals wore. Quite a few had elderly faces like chamali.

Suzy kept close to Scratch, and she whispered, 'Who are all these older, important-looking paxteys here tonight?'

'They are leaders from all the other warrens across the country.'

'Well, I'll be a monkey's uncle! I didn't think about there being paxteys in other warrens.' Suzy grinned.

'Will you be a . . . monkey's uncle?' Scratch said. 'And why will you?'

Suzy giggled. 'It's just a saying.'

Suddenly, all the chatter stopped, and two paxteys pointed across to the horizon.

'Look!'

As if someone had pressed a button, everyone looked up through the clearing in the trees.

'There!' Scratch pointed.

Suzy looked slightly to her left, and sure enough, a dark silhouette grew bigger as it headed towards them. Finally Suzy saw two sets of enormous wings. Surely they belonged to two albatrosses, but a large obstacle obscured Suzy's view. As they came closer, Suzy realised that just behind the two albatrosses was another slightly smaller albatross carrying a passenger. The warren was so quiet Suzy could hear the beat of their wings as they headed into the clearing. The two lead albatrosses landed first and quickly stepped aside for the albatross with the passenger to land directly in the middle of the clearing, and in the moonlight, Suzy saw this was Bira proudly carrying the King of all paxteys.

The King climbed down from his mount and stood in the silver glow of the moonlight for everyone to see him. Suzy knew that, being a king, he would have to look special, but she was unprepared to see anything quite as spectacular as this. His hair was shiny silver, parted in the centre, completely straight, and just touching his shoulders. He wore a rather small crown which was almost like one of Suzy's headbands, as it fitted snugly over his forehead patterns of gold and dozens of tiny diamonds sparkled in the moonlight. He seemed very old, and even though he wasn't too wrinkled, the wrinkles he had gave him a kindly look. He was clean-shaven, which was unusual, as all the elderly paxteys that Suzy had seen wore long beards. On the King's wrists were bracelets that matched his crown, and his garment of the one-piece variety that seemed to be standard for paxteys, was the deepest blue of the sea on a lovely day with veins of silver tracing through it. He was twice as tall as Scratch.

'So this is King Tobias III. Amazing' Suzy whispered.

Chamali stood up on his moss-covered chalk stone and shouted, 'Ladies and gentleman, fellow paxteys, creatures of the woodlands, His Royal Highness King Tobias III, king of all warrens in the British Isles, king of all the coves in France, king of all—'

'Yes, thank you, dear Chamali,' the King interrupted, smiling kindly. 'I think we can dispense with the long introduction today.' He looked around at the sea of faces staring back at him with love and admiration, and then he spoke. 'My dear friends of the air and the earth, ladies and gentleman—'

Slap! Slap! Slap!

King Tobias and everyone else scanned the area to see where the interruption had come from. On the pond, the catfish, their heads out of the water, were slapping the surface with their huge mouths.

'Oh! And, of course, I must not forget our friends of the water! I also notice we have a new friend who was just recently chosen, I believe. I am most pleased to meet you. I'm afraid I didn't catch your name.'

Scratch nudged Suzy, who was still smiling at the catfish, and she nearly jumped out of her skin when she realised that the King had come down from the mound where he stood and was looking straight at her. She moved towards him, her heart thumping so loudly she was sure everyone could hear it. She stepped into the moonlight and quickly and awkwardly curtsied, nearly toppling sideways as her foot caught on a long tree root.

'Oops! My name is Suzy Winnicroft, Your Majesty.' She was so nervous her voice came out in a croak.

The King shook her hand; if he had noticed her misdemeanour, he didn't show it. He greeted her with a warm smile. 'How do you do, when did you first realise you had been chosen?'

'Just yesterday morning, Your Majesty.' Had it really been only thirty-six hours since Suzy had found Scratch? *So much has happened since then*, she thought as she stared into the glowing face of His Majesty.

The King stepped back onto the mound, and Suzy moved back to Scratch and sat on a small tree stump. His Majesty glanced around at those assembled, looking very serious, as if unsure where to start.

'The subject that I am about to discuss with you today is so serious, so important that the knowledge will change your lives forever. My friends, there is a terrible sadness in the world—not just in the world that you know in and around your warren but across all warrens in the whole world. This terrible sadness is causing the clouds to burst with such force that the water creates disastrous floods, mudslides, and landslides. I know that you've experienced this even here in your own warren, through the landslides your eastern village experienced it last wintertide, when many of your friends and family were lost under the chalk and mud.'

Suzy gasped. 'Scratch, you didn't tell me about that,' she whispered.

'I haven't had the time,' Scratch whispered in response.

The King continued, 'The whole world is crying with sadness, and we must help to find the cause and put it right. Remember, this is one of the reasons that paxteys exist in the world, to help the world to be a happy and peaceful place. We are the sheriffs of the earth, of the flora and the fauna. If the clouds continue to shed such sadness through rain, hail, and snow and bring such devastating unhappiness to so many animals and humans alike, if the weather is not put back to normal, the earth will change beyond recognition.'

He paused as if to measure the audience's reaction. Old Chamali stepped forward and bowed his head.

'You wish to speak, Chamali?'

'I do indeed, Your Majesty.'

'Please do.' His Majesty nodded.

'This sadness has been building up for many years, yes?'

The King nodded once more.

'The sadness of the earth and clouds is also making the wind very angry, and there is much more thunder and lightning striking our trees. Do you have any idea at all as to the cause?'

The King thought for a few seconds and said, 'There are many theories. Paxteys with human contacts have reported that the humans are worried about it and working on the problem, too. These humans talk of things called "global warming" and "El Niño". I am sure they are doing their best, but I truly feel in my heart that the paxteys will have the answer.' He turned to look at Suzy and Scratch. 'Only when we work together with our human friends, and the creatures of the woodlands, the air, and the water, will we have an answer. I am travelling to every corner of the world and speaking in as many warrens as possible to see if an answer can be found. I will leave you now to ponder and plan a solution to this most tragic of problems, for I am going across the Atlantic to North America with Bira and my trusted guards.'

He stood for a moment smiling and waving to the crowd, and then he climbed onto Bira, who gently took off from the clearing with the other two albatrosses close behind. Within a few seconds, they were just three specks across the moon to the west.

The crowd stood for a long time, each person staring into the distance in disbelief. Gradually, whispers broke the silence, and before long, everyone was talking at once. They had so much to talk about so many questions.

Chamali stood up and clapped his hands. 'Friends, may I have your attention?' He waited for everyone to calm down. 'Now that we have heard this worrying news, we have much to think about and discuss. I am sure all the leaders from other warrens will want to be away to see your own families, so I suggest we all meet again in three moon turns. Please feel free to leave when you are ready. I wish you all well.' Scratch whispered to Suzy 'that means three months'

There was a loud hum like a swarm of bees and dozens of paxteys shot into the air and disappeared. Suzy gasped at the sight.

'That is so spooky.'

Scratch chuckled but then turned to Chamali, who had called for everyone's attention again.

'As you know,' Chamali said, 'I can always be found here, and I am always available to anyone who wishes to discuss anything. Now, off you all go to your dwellings to rest, for sleep can bring us answers. Sleep well, my dear friends.'

Suzy and Scratch then turned to leave, but Suzy realised her lovely chair wasn't at the bottom of the stairs and that she would have to walk all the way up under her own power. She turned to look at Scratch who had already sensed Suzy's need.

'Just a minute,' Scratch said. 'I've got an idea.' He disappeared and came back moments later with a hollow tree branch. He then looked about let out a low whistle. In the blink of an eye, Jam, Twee, and Twig came over.

'Hello!' Suzy squealed with delight. She loved these little people; they were so kind and full of fun.

'Okay, you three, grab a piece of the branch,' Scratch instructed. 'Suzy, you sit in the middle and hold on tight.'

Suzy sat, and before she knew what was happening, she was at the top of the cliff giggling away. She stepped off the branch, and Twee, Twig, and Jam hovered and waved.

'Bye everyone!' Suzy called. 'Thank you so much. I'll see you soon!' She walked quickly towards home, Scratch flying beside her.

'The breakfast-time conversation is going to be interesting tomorrow morning,' Suzy said. 'I wonder what Nan and Grandad will have to say about it all.'

'I wonder,' Scratch said as they walked up to the front door.

Suzy yawned. 'I'm too tired to think about it now. Goodnight, Scratch.'

'Goodnight, Suzy.'

Exhausted, Suzy fell into bed and lay there for a while, bathing in the moonlight shining through the window, dreamily pondering the things she had heard and seen. As sleep finally started to take over, she saw King Tobias, shrouded in silver mist and smiling. 'You can help us; I know you can help us.'

Chapter 5

The Little Summer House

The next day, Suzy went out to the garden after breakfast and sank onto the sun lounger, swinging to and fro, deep in thought. She had had a very serious discussion over breakfast with Grandad and Nan. Nan tut-tutted at the thought of a twelve-year-old child being saddled with such responsibility, but Grandad said Nan's worry was utter nonsense, for the experience would be educational for Suzy, arguing that it was about time she saw the serious side of life.

'When I was twelve, I was already earning a living! Nobody thought I was too young for responsibility. I had to give my wages to my old mum to help the family.'

From there he gave Suzy a long talk about how people's ignorance had brought about the terrible smog in London and other cities, how those that knew better cared only about making money and not about the environment, and how it was up to the people of Suzy's generation to put the earth right.

As Suzy rocked slowly, she realised she felt strange, as though the Suzy of two days ago had disappeared. When her eyes had opened this morning after a very heavy sleep, she had slowly looked round and contemplated the posters of S Club 7 on the walls of her room, her teddies, and the knick-knacks on the shelves and dressing table. They seemed to belong to someone else. After all the amazing things she had seen, all the new friends she had made, and the sad stories she had heard, all those belongings now appeared to be rather too juvenile for her.

Of course, she reasoned, the King had laid the responsibility on all the paxteys, not just on her and Scratch, but somehow, she felt entirely responsible.

And where is Scratch? Suzy wondered as she looked around. 'Everything really does feel very odd today.' She sighed. 'And that's another thing,' she said to herself, still fretting, 'I have to go back to school the day after tomorrow. How on earth can I be expected to go off saving the world then? I have to find out as much as I can about this global warming thing that the King mentioned so I can find out what it means and how it affects humans and paxteys. I have so much to learn and lots of research to do. I'll enjoy it, but where do I start?' She let out a deep sigh.

'The library!' she exclaimed, sitting up quickly. 'As soon as I start school, I'll go straight to the library and will book a computer for the lunchtime break so I can search the Internet. Really, where on earth is Scratch?'

Scratch hadn't joined them for breakfast, which was very unusual, as Nan said he joined her and Grandad most days. Suzy hadn't seen him since last night.

'I might find him down at the cliff,' she mumbled to herself. 'It is such a lovely day.'

Grandad had said it was unusually warm for that time of year, but she decided to pop upstairs to get her jacket just in case.

Once she had got it, she ran downstairs, 'Just going for a walk, Nan! Won't be long!' she called as she dashed outdoors.

When Suzy reached the cliff, she looked out to sea. 'Mmm, nice,' she murmured. It really was a lovely day. It seemed as if all the big ships on the horizon were travelling in single file. Closer inland, she heard the steady hum of the engines of the smaller fishing boats as they made their way into the harbour and the squawks of flocks of seagulls overhead. Above that glittering sea, Suzy sat on the bench almost at the cliff's edge and scanned the warren below, but all she could see was the tops of the trees. Even though they hadn't grown their leaves yet, she still couldn't see to the forest floor. She tried to imagine all the paxteys down there. What would they be doing now?

She looked high up at the gulls going about their business in their seagull world. A huge queen bee buzzed past her face. *First one this year,* she thought. *That's it, isn't it? Animals and human alike are going about their business and living their lives the best way they know how.*

Birds, insects, and other animals foraged for food and took it back to their homes to feed themselves and their families, just humans worked hard and shopped for their food and clothing. Everything and everybody was busy doing what they needed to do to survive. Suzy realised that people all thought that what was happening out there in the world really was for someone else to worry about, as the problem was too big for one person to solve, and they found it easier to ignore it. That is, until they couldn't ignore it—until they experienced a flood or earthquake or other disaster. Then everyone shouted, 'Why doesn't someone do something?'

'Phew!' Suzy said. 'This is heavy stuff. I always have the most amazing thoughts when I sit up here on these cliffs.'

Now that she knew the secret of what was down in the warren, Suzy wondered if she was being influenced by it somehow.

'Boo!' Scratch suddenly appeared in front of her, hovering over the edge of the cliff.

'Oh, you . . . ! I nearly fell off this bench with fright. I wish you wouldn't do that.'

'I've actually been here for some time, but you seemed so far away that I thought I would leave you alone for a while.'

'I certainly was far away. I've been having thoughts so different from usual.' Suzy glanced along the cliff and saw a lady and a dog coming towards them. She turned back to Scratch. 'Hey, you'd better hide.' She pointed to the lady.

'It's all right,' Scratch said. 'She won't be able to see me, but maybe you had better not talk to me until she's gone, otherwise she'll think you're talking to yourself.' He smiled.

Suzy giggled and stared out to sea until the lady had passed by.

When it was safe to speak, Suzy continued, 'I've been thinking of how I can find out more about global warming. She told Scratch about her plan to use the internet at her school library

'What's a library?' Scratch asked.

'It's a place full of books and computers as well.'

'And these computers will give you information?'

'I hope so, I really do,' Suzy replied. 'It's a very good place to start, anyway. And where have you been all morning?'

'I've been in the warren asking questions,' Scratch replied.

'Did you speak with Chamali?'

'Yes. I also spoke to some of the other older paxteys, and it seems that they have known something was wrong for a long while. They have done their best to protect and care for nature, which is paxteys' duty, but they have been unable to change anything. They need the King's permission.' Scratch took a deep breath.

'You see,' he continued, 'paxteys have magical powers to carry out this duty, but they are not allowed to interfere with anything, be it natural or man-made, at a worldwide level. So all they have been able to do about global warming, until now, was to watch and listen.' He then whispered mysteriously, 'And I was watching and listening as well'

'What have you been watching and listening to?' Suzy asked.

'Listening to the wind and the birds and watching all the animals.'

'How can that tell us anything?' Suzy said a little impatiently.

Scratch sighed and calmly explained, 'Wild animals live their lives by the seasons, but they are not told, "its spring, time to start building your nest." They know instinctively. Paxteys have instincts, too, although theirs are different to those of other wild animals. Paxteys can listen to the air and hear how it feels, and they've known that something is wrong and also can sense that it's getting worse. Our senses, especially our hearing and sight, are more acute than humans and most other animals', and our sixth sense is also much stronger, allowing us to pick up information on the airwaves, with techniques you humans would call sonar. The messages paxteys are receiving from the airwaves now tell us that something is very wrong with the world of the paxteys. Some paxteys have gone very bad.'

Suzy stared at Scratch nervously. 'You're scaring me. Have you talked with Chamali about this?'

'Of course, Chamali and some of my other freinds were all in a deep discussion when I noticed you sitting here. Come. We will go back to the house now.' With that, Scratch zoomed off, and Suzy trotted along behind him, deep in thought.

The paxtey are such lovely, caring creatures, and the world they protect is magical. How could anything go wrong with it?

After lunch, Suzy and Scratch sat out in the garden, and Suzy once again fired questions at Scratch, for she was desperate to understand how any paxteys could be bad and one of them or some of them are causing all the terrible disasters in the world. They were all special creatures, 'sheriffs of the earth, of the flora and fauna', as the King said.

'You know, Scratch, I've been thinking, I find it hard to believe that there could be such a thing as a bad paxtey. Something or someone must have caused their bad behaviour. They didn't just burst out of their chrysalises on the full moon and say, "This season, I'm gonna be bad!" 'said in a deep growly voice for effect.

Scratch laughed at Suzy's impression of a bad paxtey.

'Besides,' Suzy went on, 'how can a few dodgy paxteys make the whole world's climate go wrong?'

'Good question. This is where we come in. We are going to do some travelling.'

'Travelling? What do you mean?'

'Chamali told me this morning that the only way to find out anything is to venture farther afield and speak to people, paxteys, and animals to gather information and, eventually, solve our problem,' Scratch answered, a little apprehensively, Suzy thought.

'I have a funny feeling I'm not going to like what's coming next,' she muttered to herself.

'So,' Scratch went on, 'I thought we could try a short journey this afternoon to another warren that I've been to in the past, on the coast not far from Brixham in Devon.' He was smiling expectantly now. 'It's called Doyley Dell.'

Suzy's eyes went wide as she listened. 'Well, now, that's a good idea, Scratch. Just one thing you seem to have forgotten, I can't fly. How am I supposed to come with you?'

Scratch was grinning. 'That isn't a problem. Follow me'

He hovered in front of the puzzled Suzy as she stood up and put her half-finished glass of lemonade safely out of harm's way and started off down the garden path, going past the pond, through the rose arch, and to the summer house, which, much to Suzy's surprise, looked very pretty, as Grandad had repaired it and painted it cream and green. It was only a small summerhouse. It seemed as if grandad had built it by putting walls around a garden bench, and it had just small open squares instead of windows on either side of the doorway, which had no door. The window frames were made of tree branches twisted to match the arch in the doorway, and the knots and lumps on the twisted wood stood out under a fresh coat of varnish. Suzy stepped in and sat on the built-in bench spanning one wall.

'It is the prettiest little summer house I have ever seen,' she whispered proudly.

She looked out a window at the birds drinking from Grandad's pond.

'Don't get comfortable, Suzy. We're not here to relax and watch the wildlife today,' Scratch said. 'If you look to either side, you will notice there are safety bars.'

'So there are!' Suzy squealed.

'There is also a gate in front of you. Would you press that button?'

Suzy pressed a button under the window frame, and a gate slid across the doorway.

'And please pick up that bar on the floor.'

Suzy did as she was told and laid the bar, a safety harness, across her lap. It clicked into place on either side of the bench.

'That will keep you from falling off the bench, but you should hold on to the bars on the wall.'

'What on earth is all this about? Does Grandad know what you've done to his summer house?'

'Your grandad was the one that installed this equipment. This is what we were doing while you and Nan were shopping yesterday,' Scratch said with a grin.

'You sneaky devils.' Suzy chuckled.

'Now, when I say go, I want you to tap your foot once and say "away" very firmly.'

'Okay,' Suzy whispered. 'I'm feeling a bit jittery now.'

'Don't worry.' Scratch said with a smile. 'You'll be fine, 'Right. Go!' he shouted.

Suzy jumped with fright, stamped her foot, and screamed.

Scratch fell on the floor with laughter.

Suzy just held on to the safety bar looking quite disgusted. 'Well, I don't think that's very funny. You scared me nearly to death!'

Scratch rolled about on the floor, still in hysterics. 'Oh, dear!' he said finally, getting up and wiping tears from his eyes. He rose in the doorway to Suzy's eye level. 'Right, we'll just try it out first.'

Suzy groaned. 'Here goes.' She tapped her foot. 'Away!' she said firmly.

The summer house rose in the air and hovered several feet above the ground. Suzy gripped the rails nervously. As the little house rose up so did Suzy's voice

'Now what?' she shouted.

'Tell it where to go.'

'To Doyley Dell!' Suzy yelled.

With that, the house rose high above Nan's house and flew in pace with Scratch.

'Yes!' Suzy shouted. 'This is brill! Wahoo! What a way to travel.' She laughed.

'I knew you would like it!' Scratch called back.

Suzy peered out the window and let out a yelp. 'We're up so high; my stomach's turned right over!'

'Just make sure you stay in your seat and hold on. Now come on, house!' Scratch called.

The house picked up speed with a quiet wh-o-o-o-sh.

Suzy watched the clouds roll by the window. Looking down, she saw the faraway fields cut up in little squares and the rivers that looked like lines painted with glitter where the sun caught the water. As they passed a flock of seagulls, Suzy caught the eye of one of the birds, and he left his friends to sit on the window ledge.

'Caw caw! Look at me! I can fly faster than you!' he called to his friends. They just ignored him and flew on, so he jumped off and re-joined the flock.

Suzy watched all this with great interest and whispered to herself, 'Every day there's something new and just bloomin' brilliant to experience.' Then she heard a loud whirring noise, or was it a whistling noise? Or was it a jet noise?

Jet noise! 'Oh my God!' she screamed. 'It's a jumbo jet!'

'It's all right, Suzy. They can't see you.'

'Can't see me? That's even worse!' she shrieked with fright.

Scratch flew into the house, sat next to her, and patted her hand to calm her down. 'Suzy, the house will keep out of its way. You must try not to worry; we will not let anything happen to you. Just relax and enjoy.'

'Ok Phew! Look, I'm shaking.'

'You're perfectly safe.' Scratch smiled and flew outside to continue leading the way.

As the plane passed, a little boy watching out the window waved, and Suzy waved back. She wondered how it was that this boy could see her and decided to ask Scratch about that later.

Only a short time had passed, it seemed, before the little house slowed down and descended. Suzy saw the sea not far away, bordered by earth that had changed to a fiery red.

We must be in Devon. It's amazing that we've arrived so quickly, she thought.

Lower and lower went the little house, and up and up came a hillside and trees, and then, *thump*, the summer house landed.

'Hello?' called Scratch. 'Come on, Suzy, we've got to go, This way.'

'Thank you, little house,' Suzy called as she ran after Scratch.

So this is Doyley Dell, she thought. *It looks almost like a different country.* In addition to the trees that Suzy was used to seeing, she saw tall, wavy ones that looked very much like palm trees here and there. She followed Scratch into a clearing where a group of paxteys were sitting on stones shaped like armchairs. All these paxteys had beards and spoke with a slightly different accent to Suzy. Instead of *yes*, they said *arr*, fascinated; she listened as Scratch introduced himself and Suzy and then brought up last night's meeting with King Tobias.

'Have you noticed any changes?' Suzy asked.

'Arr, arr,' they said in unison, nodding.

'Do you remember, Syo?' one paxtey said, turning to the one he called Syo. 'I said to you, didn't I? I said there's been a strange ol' sound on the wind.'

Syo nodded. 'Arr. Those ol' trees over there had stood there for two hundred years they did. Then last winter came the terrible winds and the rain that went on so long when we should have had snow and uprooted the trees, and they crashed down on the dwellings, they did. Some of the folks we saved, but some were squished in the mud, never to be found.' He shook his head sadly, and the entire group said, 'Arr,' and shook their heads.

There was one that they called Leo, who seemed to be their leader, he shook his head too. He looked at Scratch and Suzy. 'It's on the air, you know. Arr, we've heard the voices.'

'Whose voices?' Suzy asked.

'Well, now, that we don't know.'

'Could it be the voices of other paxteys?' Scratch asked.

'Well, now,' Leo answered, 'I couldn't say. Syo over there thought he heard a voice say "heat", and me, well, I thought I heard a voice say "crush", but we can't be sure. If you stand quiet on a still day, you'll hear . . . Something . . .' He became wistful.

'Will I be able to hear it?' Suzy enquired.

Everyone turned to look at Suzy, who had perched herself on a fallen tree trunk.

'Well, now, I can't say that you will and I can't say that you won't,' Leo said, 'but as you are one of the chosen? Mmm, you might.'

'I see,' Suzy said, puzzled. Scratch rolled his eyes, indicating that they weren't going to get much help here.

'You will hear, Suzy, and you will know,' a voice said.

'Huh? Where did that voice come from?' Suzy said. 'Scratch, did you hear it'?

'Yes, and it came from that direction.' Scratch pointed to the tree behind her.

Suzy edged slowly towards it and looked up to one of the large lower branches. A kestrel perched there stared at her.

'Hello?' she called to the bird.

'Hello,' he answered.

'Was that you speaking just then?'

'Yes. I was eavesdropping, and I wanted you to know that you will hear and see many things, and you will eventually find the answers, but for now, you must learn everything that Scratch will teach you. Along the way, you will make many friends, but beware of the ones who pretend.'

'Pretend? Pretend to do what?' Suzy was puzzled.

'Beware of those who pretend to be your friends. You must learn how to tell the good seed from the bad.'

'Oh, I see.' *At least I think I do*, she thought.

'I have to say goodbye now. We will meet again!' the kestrel called as he took off into the air.

'Ah, how beautiful,' Suzy said, 'To have a chat with a kestrel; that really is something else!'

'Something else?' Scratch asked.

'It's just a saying.' Suzy smiled.

Scratch sighed. 'Will I ever get used to these strange sayings? But then, if you can adjust to my world, then I will do my best to get used to your language.'

They walked back to the other paxteys, who had been watching with interest. They drank the drinks they were offered, thanked the paxteys for their hospitality, and headed back to the summer house.

Suzy stepped in, closed the gate, sat down, buckled the safety bar, and held on. 'Away!' she said firmly.

Slowly the Little House rose, and all the paxteys from Doyley Dell rose with it as they waved and said their farewells. When they reached the top of the dell, whoosh! The house took off, and Suzy and Scratch were on their way back to Capel.

That was incredible, Suzy thought. She wondered why Scratch didn't sit in the house with her as they journeyed back, but then she suspected that the house was following him home.

She sighed and smiled contentedly. *Scratch really is just about the best friend anyone could ever have. Every human should have his or her own paxtey. What a wonderful place the world would be if everyone could feel as good as I do at this moment.*

It was late afternoon on this typical spring day, with the sun sitting low in the sky and a slight misty haze appearing over the sea, as the weather had been very sunny but cold. As Grandad would say, 'Looks like we're in for a frosty night tonight.'

Suzy's thoughts went back to what the kestrel had said. When she heard voices, what would they say? Would she be scared? Would she even hear anything at all?

Back at Nan's house, the little house landed so precisely in the spot where it had been before that no one would notice it had even moved. As Suzy got out, she patted the wall fondly.

'Thank you so much. That was brill.'

Suzy and Scratch dashed up the garden path just in time for tea. 'Nan just you wait till you hear where we've been!' Suzy called as she ran.

Chapter 6

At the End of the Rainbow

The next twenty-four hours passed too quickly, and before Suzy knew where she was, she was getting ready for school. She donned her uniform and prepared herself with lots of deep breathing and chanting.

'Everything's cool, everything's cool. Phew. Phew.'

She had to revert to being the Suzy Winnicroft that all her friends and teachers knew before the holiday, for if she behaved differently, everyone would wonder what was wrong and would start asking questions, but she felt so unbelievably different now that she had the responsibilities and a mission to accomplish.

'Hey. Suzy! Hiya!' Suzy's friend Julie waved when Suzy arrived on school grounds.

'Hiya!' Suzy said.

'Where have you been? I phoned yesterday, and your Nan said you were out visiting a relative. I was hoping we could do something before we had to come back.'

Suzy took a deep breath. 'Yeah, sorry, Ju. I had stuff to do, and I couldn't get out of it, but not to worry. We'll have time to do something later, eh?'

'You okay?' Julie said with concern. 'You look tired.'

'I'm fine. So what have you been doing with yourself?' Suzy asked, desperate to change the subject.

'I met up with Dee the day before yesterday, and we went over the club. We had a right laugh. That Tommy Bewly keeps looking at her. I think she's got herself a boyfriend!' She giggled.

'Woo!' replied Suzy with a pretend giggle. 'Did you have a dance?'

'Yeah, there was a load of us, Janet Scholes, Jimmy Goodhue, and all that lot. Oh, I wish you had come.'

'I'll try to get there next week, maybe.' *Oh! I've got to get up to the library*, Suzy remembered. 'I have to run up and sign in.'

'I've done it already,' Julie replied. 'Hey, there's Jan over there. I'll see you in class, then, right?'

'Okay,' Suzy said, breathing a sigh of relief as Julie dashed off.

She took the stairs to the library two at a time.

'Where's the fire Winnicroft?' called Mrs Henwick, the head of year. 'We don't want accidents on the first day back, do we?'

'Sorry Mrs Henwick.' Suzy slowed down till she was out of sight of the teacher and then walked almost at running speed.

'It'll be too late to book a computer in a minute,' she muttered. A couple of students were already waiting in the library entrance when she arrived, but Suzy's turn soon came.

'Can I book a PC for twelve to one-thirty, please?'

'The whole of the lunchtime?' the library assistant asked.

'Yes, please,' Suzy said firmly.

'Okay. Suzy Winnicroft,' the assistant said as she wrote it in the book.

'Right, see you later!' Suzy dashed off to class.

As she walked into the room, most of her classmates were already there talking in small groups, some giggling, others whispering and peering over their shoulders, obviously gossiping about others in the room.

Just two weeks ago I would have been enjoying a good old chit chat with my freinds and now it doesn't seem so important anymore, Suzy thought.

'Suzy, over here,' Julie called.

Suzy looked across the room to where all her closest school friends sat together. 'Hiya. You all right, you lot?' she said as she joined them.

In no time at all, double maths and double English had taken care of the morning. At break time, Suzy was her usual self, and her friends had stopped asking questions. Then, at lunch break, Suzy ate her sandwich quickly on her way to the library and then settled down in front of the PC.

'Right, here we go,' she said to herself. 'I need to log on, and my search term is . . . global warming?' She typed it in and pressed Enter, and there were pages and pages of information.

'Phew! I thought this was going to be difficult.' She looked over to see if the printer was busy.

'I can't write all this down. I'll get it all printed off so I can study it properly at home and show it to Scratch. Hmm . . . I wonder if Scratch can read. Here we are. Print.'

After that, she couldn't wait for the day to finish as she sat through a session of social studies and another of art. At last she was on her way home with Julie wishing she could run but careful to do what was expected of her.

Julie, you're my best friend, and I wish I could tell you everything, she thought I *would love to share this amazing adventure with you, but I can't. Who knows? Maybe things will be different soon.*

By then Suzy had arrived at the turning to her lane and home.

'Bye, Ju! See you tomorrow!'

'Okay, Su! See ya! Byee!'

Suzy glanced back to see Julie watching her go off down the lane. Suzy had also borrowed some reference books from the library and from class, as many as she could carry, and Julie examined her bags full of books and files. She must have been curious but probably thought it wasn't a good idea to ask what they were for, Suzy guessed. Besides, even though she had been preoccupied all day, she did have a reputation for being a bit of a bookworm. Her true friends understood that her books and her studies were important part of her and wouldn't think it unusual for her to walk home so loaded up.

That evening after dinner, Suzy and Scratch studied all the information Suzy had bought home. With the pages spread across the dining table, Suzy read and made notes for further exploration and for discussion. Scratch hovered above the table and picked out certain pages that particularly interested him (and yes, he could read).

'Listen to this, Scratch: "Each year in the UK, experts estimate, air pollution speeds up the deaths of 8,000 people who are already ill, and another 10,500 UK citizens go into hospital with breathing problems because of exposure to air pollution." 'She sighed in frustration, 'So much to learn. There's information on weather fronts, great storms like hurricanes, the greenhouse effect.' She picked up another printout.

'There is a hole in the ozone layer over the Antarctic measuring . . . as much as twenty-six *million* square kilometres! Geez! Can you believe that? And this says that global temperatures have risen, causing the climate to change worldwide!

She looked up at Scratch. 'Are these the answers we're looking for? Here it says that the world's top scientists are working on the ozone-layer problem and that the ozone layer is showing signs of repairing itself and will continue to do so as long as the world's heads of state stick to current programs phasing out CFCs until they're banned entirely. I think Chamali may find some of this interesting.

The next few days passed quickly. Suzy continued to learn as much as she could about the world's weather patterns, and Scratch joined her every now and then to pass on news from the warren, although, unfortunately, there wasn't much. Suzy continued to wonder why on earth she had been chosen to help; she couldn't see how anything she did could possibly make a difference.

It was a rainy Sunday afternoon, Suzy was lying face down on her bed listening to her favourite band through her earphones as usual when Scratch flew in through the window.

'Suzy, wake up! Wake up!' She didn't answer. 'Suzy, wake *up*!' he shouted, and then he spotted the earphones. He flew over and pushed them off of her head. 'Come on!' he shouted.

Suzy shot up off the bed in a fright, throwing a pillow at Scratch, who quickly flew sideways to dodge it. He laughed.

'Oooh! You made me jump again!' Suzy squealed. 'What is it?'

'Go to the window and listen,' Scratch said.

She opened the window wide, looked out, and listened. Some big black clouds still sat in the sky behind the house, but the rain had stopped and the sun had broken through, and straight ahead over the horizon was a huge rainbow. Then she heard a sound almost like a siren but much gentler, more like a flute than a horn. It surrounded her and gradually filled her head.

'Can you hear it?' Scratch said excitedly.

'Yes. What is it?' The sound grew louder and louder.

'Hurry and get ready to go out. It's the little ones.'

Suzy jumped to action grabbing her shoes and jacket. 'What little ones?'

'Hurry up and I'll show you.'

Suzy ran downstairs and scribbled a note to Nan, as Suzy didn't want to wake her from her forty winks, and then she ran out of the house, muttering to herself, 'Now what's Scratch getting me into?' She put on her shell jacket as she ran to the edge of the garden and called out to Scratch, 'Where are we going?'

'You will need to get in the little house, as we have to get to the bottom of the cliff and to the other end of the rainbow in a hurry.'

'Huh? What do you mean the other end of the rainbow?'

'You'll see.' Scratch smiled.

Suzy ran to the summer house. 'Hello, little house!' she said, and then she closed the gate, sat down, lowered the safety bar, and called, 'Away!' Up went the house, and hovering above the garden as it waited to be told its destination.

'The other end of the rainbow!' Scratch called.

Whoosh! The little house was away and above the cliffs in no time.

We're going out to sea, Suzy thought, but no, the house changed direction and headed to the western end of the warren. *We really are heading towards the end of the rainbow. This is really strange.*

When the house entered the rainbow, it wasn't anything like Suzy had imagined from a distance. The colours were clearly differentiated into individual colours, but within each colour, she could see the millions and trillions of tiny water droplets lit up by the sun, glistening turquoise and mauve and blue, and there were red and yellow. Suzy put her arms out to feel the damp air.

'Woo-hoo! I'm touching a rainbow!' she called to Scratch.

Bright colours engulfed the house as it descended, following Scratch along the curve of the rainbow almost to the end, where they diverted to a small grassy patch between bushes and trees. As Suzy stepped out, she heard the joyful sound of paxtey voices singing.

Scratch laughed and flew in the direction of the sound and then back to Suzy. 'Come on, Suzy! This way quickly!'

Excited, she ran after him, but at the end of the pathway, she nearly tripped over a young paxtey. The Paxtey's were everywhere along the footpath, hovering in the air, and flying to and fro. All of them were singing:

Welcome, welcome little ones,

Very welcome you've become;

We will care for you,

We will cherish you,

In our arms, we will love you,

Until mature and grown are you.

All the paxteys standing on the ground moved aside to make way for a procession. Chamali, at the head, waved happily and smiled, and twelve other paxteys followed him, hovering two by two. Suzy thought they were female, as they had long hair that was carefully combed and held back with hair slides that looked as if they were made from shells and their softer facial features were much more feminine. They were also more mature, motherly in manner than the other paxteys Suzy had met, but maybe not quite as old as Chamali. She followed the procession to—wonders of wonders!—The end of the rainbow. It was vibrating with colour where it met the ground, and as Suzy moved closer to it, she could feel the pulsations on her skin more intensely. This felt electric. When she stepped into the rainbow's end, the colours glowed all around her, and there at the centre was a golden light. She remembered Grandad's words: 'Find the end of the rainbow and you will find a crock of gold.'

Scratch hovered alongside her. 'Do you see them, Suzy?' he asked excitedly.

She peered through the colours to see a giant basket bathed in the golden light sitting on the ground. In the basket were twelve paxtey babies no more than three inches long, each wrapped in a shawl woven in golden thread.

'Oh my,' Suzy whispered.

'The gold in the crock is actually paxtey babies! They are so sweet!'
She said as the twelve paxteys in the procession each lovingly lifted a
baby, turned, and slowly retraced their steps along the well-trodden path.
As they returned to the heart of the warren, they continued their song:

> Welcome, welcome, little ones,
>
> Welcome, welcome, you've become;
>
> We will care for you, cherish you,
>
> In our arms, we will love you,
>
> Until mature and grown are you.
>
> As best we can we will
>
> Protect you from harm;
>
> You must never know fear or alarm.
>
> Until a chrysalis you will be
>
> And a new life you will see.

Scratch explained that they would be cared for in a special nursery as
he and Suzy followed the procession. Suzy glanced back for another look
at the rainbow, still finding it hard to believe that those babies had come
from there. Then the rainbow disappeared, and everything appeared to
have gone back to normal.

Eventually the singing stopped at a huge mound with a giant willow
tree growing from it. Several paxteys flew above the mound and the
willow tree, where they flew back and forth, creating a wave of pink and
blue light. Slowly the tree moved, revealing a large wooden door in the
mound. Suzy peered inside after the paxteys had gone in to see a nursery
with twelve cots. Not only did they have nurses to take care of their
personal needs, but they also had four paxteys guarding them at all times.

Suzy was fascinated as she walked back to the little house, asking questions all the way.

'You see,' Scratch explained, 'Paxteys aren't like humans. We don't have mothers and fathers, husbands and wives. Once a year, babies are delivered to the rainbow, as you have seen today. Sometimes there is only one baby; other times there are as many as twelve, as there were today.'

'Where do they come from?' Suzy said.

'From the Great One in the Mist, who lives somewhere far away? We don't question it we just know that at a certain time of year, the horn sounds to tell us it's time to collect the little ones at the rainbow.'

Suzy headed back to the summer house in the clearing, 'I'd better get home. Nan and Grandad weren't expecting me to be away today.' Scratch followed, having a quiet chat with Chamali. *Is he coming along, too?* Suzy wondered

'So this is the summer house, Very smart.' Chamali smiled.

Suzy sat inside and closed the safety gate with a proud smile on her face. She was glad he approved of her unusual mode of transport. Her mind then wandered back to the babies. *I've just seen baby paxteys! Aha!* She chuckled and called out, 'Away!' The house took off and hovered above the trees, waiting for further instructions. Suzy looked out to sea. *I've never seen the bay from this angle before*, she thought.

'Forward slowly!' she instructed, and the house headed out to sea. The sun was shining, sparkling on the white surf.

'Tide's in,' she called out to Scratch.

'Suzy, where are you going?' Scratch asked, hanging on the door frame, 'I thought you needed to get back.'

'I just wanted to see what it was like to fly over the sea,' she said. She looked down at a group of cormorants bobbing on the water, taking turns to dive for food.

'Little house, go up higher, please.' The house rose higher and higher until Suzy could no longer see the cormorants.

'Stop!' she instructed. There the house hovered, and the view was beautiful. She looked across the bay and then across the sea at the large lump of land spreading as far as her eye could see—France. The patch of sea between the Warren and Folkestone, Dover and France looked so small now. She looked back at the cliffs and further inland at all those tidy squares of farmer's fields and sighed at the wonder of it all.

Suzy couldn't believe that one day this could all be different; it could all have vanished underwater because of the greenhouse effect, as all the books and websites had said.

Suzy reminded herself that the world's scientists were working hard to make sure that didn't happen, but in the meantime, she had to do everything she could do, no matter how small the effort.

'Every little bit helps,' she murmured. 'There I go again! I always have the most amazing thoughts when I'm looking out to sea.'

'That's because the peaceful view helps you ponder,' Chamali said, who had come to sit next to Suzy.

Suzy jumped, surprised to see him, but then became calm again as she and her two favourite paxteys sat, staring out to sea, enjoying the peaceful view and their private thoughts.

Then Suzy broke the silence again. 'How long will those baby paxteys have to stay in the nursery, Chamali?'

'They are cared for in the nursery until they are about two years old and able to start their lessons with me and to learn all other skills from the older paxteys just by spending time with them,' he replied.

'How long does that take?'

'Just as with humans, I'd venture, some young ones are brighter than others and learn quickly whereas others take much longer to learn the same things. Nevertheless, it takes many years for a paxtey to be ready to hibernate as an adult.' Chamali went on to explain that after the first hibernation, paxteys began caring for and keeping watch over the wild animals and the vegetation in the warren and also in the sea it bordered.

Suzy sat and thought about this for a moment. 'But, Chamali, what happens during your hibernation, since that lasts three months and is often in the worst weather?'

Chamali smiled, clearly pleased that Suzy was taking such an interest. 'Aaah, but we don't *all* hibernate at once. No, each paxtey hibernates every other year; they plan this very carefully with other paxteys. So, you see, there are always paxteys to keep watch.'

'I see,' Suzy said with a frown, for this confused her. 'Scratch, you told me you never sleep except during hibernation. How can you go two years without sleep?'

'Well, I must get back and see that the little ones have been settled,' Chamali said. 'I'll leave you to answer the rest of Suzy's questions, Scratch.' With a smile, and a wave he was gone.

Suzy turned and looked at Scratch expectantly.

'We do rest, and it's a kind of sleep, I suppose. As you spend more time with us, you will notice that every now and then, one of us will find a cosy little spot to sit and rest and close our eyes, but our senses are alert at all times.'

Suzy was on a roll now, and more and more questions popped into her head. 'How old were you when you first hibernated?' she asked.

'Paxteys do this when we know we need to rather than at a set age. I was about eighteen of your human years when I had my first one, and I have had three hibernations now.'

'What?' Suzy was shocked. She stared at him, her brain buzzing. 'If you were eighteen for your first hibernation that means you had the second one when you were twenty, making you *twenty-two*!' She squealed.

'Why is that such a surprise?' Now Scratch was puzzled.

'I just presumed we were, erm, well . . . somehow I just thought that we were the same age.'

'You need to understand that paxteys age much more slowly than humans. You can see this if you consider Chamali's case. He is around two hundred of your years but seems to be about the same age as your grandad.'

'I understand now . . . I think.'

'The hardest part about hibernating is finding somewhere dry, warm, and safe,' Scratch continued. 'Not all of us choose to stay with humans. Some stay in their home warrens, where other paxteys watch over them. I was very fortunate to find your grandparents, as they knew about paxteys before they met me and welcomed me into their home, as they are watchers. Unlike chosen ones, they don't take part in warren activities, but they do help us paxteys.'

'I see,' Suzy said. 'And what about the, erm, end. You know?' She nodded at Scratch, hoping he would understand what she meant.

Scratch did not. 'What end?'

'You know, when you . . . die?'

'Ah, well, once again, it is certainly not the same as a human death. We just cease.'

'What do you mean? You just stop breathing or something?'

'Oh, no. once we reach the end of our time, we know it, and we just puff out, vanish, and disappear.'

'Geez! That's terrible! So one minute I could be talking to you and the next you'd be gone?'

'No, no.' Scratch chuckled at Suzy's horrified face. 'For one thing, I've got to get much older before that happens, and for another, we do get to say farewell before we go. What's more, paxteys never get ill, so I don't think you need worry about my going just yet. But you're right that once we know it is time to go, that's it; there's nothing we can do to stop it.' His expression became very serious. 'There is one reason that paxteys may puff out before he's old.'

'What's that?'

'It may happen if he's done something so unacceptably bad, so terribly wrong that he is so full of remorse and shame that he cannot live with himself. Then he would cease to be. He would receive no judgement from other paxteys; he would just know it was time to go, and he would go.' Scratch's face became sad, and he sighed.

Suzy shook her head in amazement. She had never had to think about life and death much, and like most twelve-year-olds, she took life for granted. The most she ever thought about it was that her mum had brought her into the world and that one day a long way off she would die and that would be that. She thought the paxtey way was just magic.

CHAPTER 7

Ogystone

Many, many miles away from Capel-le-Ferne, way up in the icy north, was a place called the Isle of Misty Fear, named by a tough pirate in the eighteenth century who accidentally came across it whilst trying to outrun an English frigate.

The bravest of the brave could not stay on the island for longer than a few hours. The mist, thick grey-green smog that smelled like boiling mildew and bones, never cleared. Even more disturbing were the sounds that came from the mist—heart-rending wailing and evil whispers followed by gloating guttural laughter. The Isle was indeed a terrible place that no one would ever visit twice.

In the centre of the island, covered in snow, with giant icicles hanging from every ledge and precipice, stood Ogystone Mountain, where, at the peak of the mountain just off centre, it was possible to see a tiny trail of smoke trickling into the atmosphere. There was an entrance to the mountain, but only one, a small cave that would be overlooked by the average human, for here in this sad land, in this sad mountain, lived an evil old hermit called Ogystone.

Two centuries ago, Ogystone arrived at the end of the rainbow in the capel warren along with two other paxtey babies. All the nursery paxteys believed him to be one more precious baby to join the group, and even when he emerged from the nursery, the paxteys all believed him to be one of them.

As time went by, however, it became obvious that this creature had been a mistake and was, perhaps, a freak of nature, for Ogystone was not like the other paxteys.

He hated joining in anything and never wanted to help. He didn't possess the compassion and humility of the other paxteys, and what's more, he didn't care.

At the first opportunity, he left his paxteys community behind to find a new life for himself.

The paxteys thought that he had become so full of remorse, so ashamed of himself that he had puffed out, so they sang the goodbye song and sent their love to his spirit, although some also breathed a sigh of relief, as he had become a worry to the community, for they couldn't control him, and some even feared him.

Ogystone went to live on the Isle of Misty Fear before it had a name. Then, the unmapped island was a beautiful snowy habitat where an abundance of wildlife, including sea lions, penguins, and many species of sea birds, lived out a happy existence. That ended when Ogystone arrived.

He set about clearing the island of every living creature, for he had no intention of sharing his home with any idiotic animals.

'I hate the disgusting, dirty, noisy things,' he muttered to himself as he systematically gathered them up and threw them into the sea. He stared at a huge hill of ice and visualised several giant walruses, and they appeared and roared across the island, smashing everything that moved and frightening every other living creature off into the sea and into the air. When they had finished they went back into the hill of ice and were never seen again. Finally the island was quiet. Ogystone had his wish he was alone.

Since then Ogystone had lived alone inside the mountain and was completely self-sufficient.

He was a hateful, frightening figure. At four feet tall and very fat, Ogystone was much bigger than other paxteys; had piercing, dark eyes; and wore clothing made from material that had come from some of the ships that had crashed on his island from time to time he favoured a miserable grey speckled sack outfit with black shapes. Any of the lovely hues of the rainbow that had been in his clothes and his eyes had disappeared long ago, along with his happiness and laughter and any need to care.

He rarely ventured away from the island, and then only when an opportunity to do something wicked presented itself, such as sending trees crashing down on paxtey and human dwellings, and floods and other disasters brought him great joy. And when he was on the island, he spent his miserable life planning further destruction and despair from his bumpy stone chair, which matched the huge warts on his face and hands so that an observer could barely tell where the chair ended and Ogystone began.

Deep in the mountain were many chambers in which he grew and stored food, including toadstools and many other fungi and mosses and his special green weed, and water to nourish the plants and himself from the melting snow hundreds of feet above on the mountaintop. The water made its way to Ogystone's home by dripping down through many layers of soil and limestone and other rock. The water had also carved out the ledges and chambers he used for storage and his dwelling. To harvest his food, Ogystone had enticed paxteys onto the island and made them his slaves.

Although Ogystone had enjoyed being alone for a while, once he had his slaves, he soon discovered that it was good to have underlings, for he could kick them about whenever the whim struck him. Two such paxteys, Kurr and Kree, his favourites, sat on either side of him in the cave and accompanied him everywhere he went, although that wasn't very far now he had an army of several hundred paxtey slaves, so many that he'd lost count. He chuckled quietly to himself whenever he thought of how he enticed them into his service.

Each time disaster struck a paxtey dwelling place, some paxteys disappeared, and all the other paxteys believed that they had puffed out from the shock of their inability to do anything to stop the disaster, but they hadn't puffed out at all. Ogystone had made them invisible and carried them off to be his slaves.

Then, back on the Isle of Misty Fear, Ogystone forced them to drink juice made from the special green weed that grew around the pools in the mountain caves, making them believe it would help them recover. However, the terrible truth was that it made them forget where they had come from and who they were, and they became subservient, deriving their only glimmer of happiness from pleasing Ogystone. As their memories faded, so did the rainbow colours in and around their bodies.

Their eye colour faded first, then their nails, and then their skin until they were left a dirty brown and their clothes became ragged.

He laughed a maniacal laugh. 'It makes me joyful to see such misery! Especially from all those namby-pambies with their keep-this-nice, keep-that-pretty, mustn't-hurt, must-be-caring attitude.' Kurr and Kree knew the secret of the green weed but would never tell anyone. Sometimes they all cackled and crowed along with their master.

What an ugly picture they made as they schemed to destroy oh-so-wonderful King Tobias and goody two-shoes Chamali.

'Just you wait till you see what I've got in store for you! Yesss!'

Chapter 8

The Voice in the Mist

The next few weeks passed quietly for Suzy, with visits from Scratch almost daily. She wandered down to the warren at every opportunity and enjoyed sitting on her special branch-and-leaf chair and quietly observing the paxteys, getting to know all the characters in the community and listening to their stories. They really were the most loveable and kind creatures she had ever met—not that she had met that many people in her twelve short years.

Suzy was beginning to think that maybe King Tobias had been overreacting about weather patterns. By now, she had found out as much as she could from her research, and it didn't seem to be of any help to anyone and she'd been thinking she might have a serious chat with Chamali as soon as she could.

On Friday afternoon, Suzy rushed home with Julie as usual.

'Don't forget, we're off to the shops tomorrow,' Julie said. 'I've got some money to spend from my birthday, and I'd like to get that CD I was telling you about.'

'Okay. What time?' Suzy asked.

'Well, we can have a bit of a lie in, so, I'll meet you at the end of the lane about half ten, yeah?'

'That'll be just right. It'll be so nice not to hear that alarm go off at six-thirty for once!' Suzy sighed.

She turned right into the lane and waved to Julie. 'Bye, Ju! See you tomorrow!'

'Bye, Su! Looks like there's a mist coming up, so mind how you go, and watch out for cars!' Julie called back before she carried on down the road.

As Suzy walked farther down the lane, sure enough, the mist was blowing in fast. The Capel mist was well known for appearing without any warning. A traveller could easily mistake it for bonfire smoke at first, as it started off wispy, but then it thickened up and engulfed everything, with the only indication of the outside world is the foghorns soulfully blowing its warning to the ships out to sea. Capel was so high above sea level that it wasn't unusual to be engulfed in clouds and sea mists on a regular basis, so Suzy wasn't bothered by it now.

All she could hear now was the sound of her shoes echoing back at her, until—

'Huh! Ha ha!'

Suzy stopped in her tracks. 'Who's there?' she called, her eyes going wide as saucers and a chill running down her back. She looked back to see if she could still see Julie, or anyone else, but through the mist, she couldn't even see the hedge that should have been right next to her.

'Ha, ha, haa. Grrr. Yesss.'

Suzy frantically looked around for the source of the deep, evil, growling voice through the mist.

'Now is the time! We arr ready, yesss! The time is right now. Hrrmm.'

Suzy screamed and ran. 'Oh my God! What the *hell* is that!' she yelled as she picked up the pace. In just a few seconds she would be at her gate. Just a few seconds. Quickly. Quickly.

'They'll see, ha! It's my time now, grr!'

'Nan, Grandad, Quick! Open the door!' Suzy plunged head first through the hole in the hedge next to the gate and ran for the back door, falling into Nan, her arms full of washing. Puffing and blowing, Suzy flung open the back door and ran in, Nan following close behind. Nan threw her washing on the table, rushed back to the door, and locked it. Suzy, gasping for breath, flung herself on a kitchen chair.

'Oh my God! Nan, what was that? Did you hear it?'

'I heard it,' Nan puffed, looking fearfully around and closing the open windows.

'For goodness sake, we've got to get all the windows and doors locked!'

'I didn't think about that!' Suzy yelled, jumping up.

'Come on, get focused and think, girl. I'll do the upstairs,' Nan shouted, sprinted for the stairs despite her creaky knees.

As Suzy moved through each of the downstairs rooms, locking everything with a latch and a bolt, she realised she couldn't remember ever seeing Nan run so fast. To close the last window in the back of the house, Suzy had to lean out into the mist to reach the latch. 'Oh no,' she whispered as she heard the voice.

'Get him! Teach him! Hrrrm!'

Suzy gasped and slammed the window shut. She then returned to the kitchen, where Nan put the kettle on for tea.

Funny how in every emergency we always put the kettle on for tea, Suzy thought. She and Nan both flopped down at the table. Nan sighed and shook her head in disbelief.

'What is it, Nan?'

'I'm sure I don't know. I've never experienced anything like this,' Nan replied.

'The voice started as the mist rolled in. It was as if the mist was talking. Oh, Nan, I was so scared,' Suzy whispered, in case whatever was speaking could hear her. 'Do you suppose everyone can hear that voice?'

I don't know; I heard it as I was getting the washing in I'm as baffled as you are.' Nan filled the teapot. 'A nice cup of strong, sweet tea will take care of the shock, I think. I'll have one with you.'

'I'm just beginning to stop shaking,' Suzy said as she took a sip of her tea.

Then they heard a knock, and Suzy jumped, spilling her tea all over the table. They both looked down just as the cat flap slowly opened but the cat was already indoors.

'Oh no now what?' Suzy groaned.

Nan just held her breath.

A tiny familiar face appeared through the cat door. 'Are you two okay?'

'Scratch, it's you! Thank goodness!' Nan smiled.

Suzy crashed down into a chair as Nan rushed to grab a cloth for the spilt tea.

'Did you hear that voice? 'Suzy whispered to Scratch

'Yes, we all heard it,' Scratch said. 'All the little ones were crying and the older folk flying about checking that everything was okay when I left.'

'It came out of the mist, Scratch. It was the mist talking!' Suzy said.

'No, it wasn't the mist talking. It was someone using the mist to send a message, to scare us all,' Scratch explained.

'Well, it certainly did that. I'm *still* shaking. Should we call the police, Nan?'

'I should imagine that if all of Capel heard the voice the police must have got dozens of phone calls by now,' Nan reasoned.

Bang, bang, bang! Someone was at the door.

Suzy screamed.

'Will someone open this door? Why is it locked?' It was Grandad.

'Oh my word, it's you!' Nan said as she opened the door, breathing a sigh of relief. She was looking decidedly ragged now.

'I was just walking home from the meeting along the cliff path when the mist came up,' Grandad said. 'You heard the voice, too, then?'

'Yes, we certainly did,' Nan said. 'Do you think everyone heard it, even people not involved with the paxteys?'

Everyone sat quietly waiting for Grandad's opinion, Scratch in his chair on the end of the table and Suzy across from him, sipping her tea with shaky hands, shifting her eyes from Scratch to Nan to Grandad.

'I think what I'll do is give ol' Bob a ring,' Grandad said, 'since he's nearest to us on the cliff road. He's not involved in the paxtey world, and he'll tell me straight away if he heard anything. I bet you one of my best marrows he hasn't.' That was quite a bet, for Grandad's best marrows were entered in the local garden show. He dialled Bob's number.

'Is that you, Bob? Yes . . . oh . . . yes . . . Got back okay. Took the cliff path, though after all these years, you'd think I'd see it coming wouldn't you? It was a thick one though, and, erm, what with all the shouting . . . You didn't?' . . . Well, I don't know who was shouting. It sounded like someone was arguing somewhere. You know how the mist carries sound . . . Yes, yes . . . Um, you okay, mate? Well, yes I know you didn't have to go anywhere. I just wondered if you thought it a bit unusual.' He listened and gave a nervous laugh. 'I suppose I am getting a bit odd in my old age . . . Okay, then, see you later.' Grandad rang off and sat down at the table.

'I think he thought I was off my rocker.' He chuckled. 'Anyway, he never heard anything, and I don't think anyone besides us and the little folk down in the warren did either. I'm just going to have a wander down the garden now to check for any damage from the mist.' Suzy knew that what Grandad really meant but wouldn't say was that he was going to go outside, stand by his shed, and listen.

'I'll come with you,' Scratch said.

'Wait for me! I'm coming too,' Suzy said.

'And wait for me,' Nan said. 'Don't you think you're leaving me on my own'

They all walked slowly down to the bottom of the garden, looking around and listening as they went. Suzy went into the little house and Nan followed her, still holding her cup of tea, and they both sat down to watch and listen. Grandad opened his shed and stood in the doorway. Scratch settled on top of the little house.

Puffs of mist still swirled about, and the air felt very cold and damp. It was so quiet that the only sounds to be heard were Nan sipping and swallowing her tea and the sorrowful tone of the foghorn in the distance.

Suzy suddenly heard a slightly different, urgent tone from a lot of horns, yet it was somehow gentle. Scratch appeared in front of her.

'Suzy, we must go immediately. We are being called.'

Nan jumped out of the little house, still holding her tea. 'Follow me!' Scratch yelled, and *whoosh*, the little house was away. Suzy held on tight.

The little house headed out across the warren, and as it descended, Suzy spotted six adult paxteys hovering in a circle and blowing into shells like they were trumpets. The sound was carried in every direction, and already dozens of paxteys were responding to the call.

Suzy landed in the clearing near Chamali's stone and looked all around before stepping out of the house; there were so many little people and animals in the clearing that she had to be careful where she walked to avoid stepping on them. She headed for her leaf-and-twig chair, made herself comfortable, and waited.

Soon, it was just like the night of the paxtey haven, with so many paxteys of all ages and creatures of the ground and air all chatting together, although today's meeting was slightly different, as there was no music, and everyone was speaking in worried tones. Suzy even noticed that some of the young ones with two nursery paxteys were crying.

Very shortly, everyone was gathered. Suzy looked up into the trees to see dozens of birds all talking at once. Sparrows chatted to the wise old owls, magpies shouted to Jays, and even a pair of hawks talked to a kestrel, and there, on a branch which spanned the clearing, was the mighty albatross Bira.

Chamali appeared and climbed to his stone so that everyone could hear him, and he introduced several elderly paxteys who, he said, cared for other communities around the country as far away as Scotland with lovely names: Heather Haven, Pine Tree Loch, Glenny Dale. Chamali said that they all had one thing in common they had all heard that terrible voice booming out of the mist at various times in the last week.

Chamali confirmed that only paxteys and those connected to them had heard the voice, so he presumed that it was exclusively a paxtey matter. He then asked the first of the elders to speak, and after that, each of the others got his turn to make some useful suggestions. The Paxteys from Glenny Dale was adamant that something evil had developed. The leader of Heather Haven would not accept that it could be anything to do with the world of the Paxtey and was concerned that somehow humans somewhere had found a way into their world. Most of the Paxteys just could not believe that it could be one of their own that would do something so evil.

By then, three hours had passed, and the sun had gone down. The nursery paxteys had taken the young ones out of the way for their rest, and many of the birds had snuggled together with their heads under their wings and fallen fast asleep. Suzy was cold, so she sneaked back into the little house, where she knew there was a jacket that she could wrap herself in to keep warm.

All too soon it was Suzy's turn to speak, as a chosen one she was entitled to have a say in the matter. Every one turned to her respectfully waiting for her opinion. Chamali smiled and nodded to her to begin.

'Well,' she said apprehensively, 'I, too, was very frightened when I heard the voice, but now I'm angry and determined to find out who is doing this. The paxteys are wonderfully kind creatures, and I find it hard to believe that the voice could be from a paxtey that has gone bad, when it goes against a paxtey's whole being to hurt anything.'

After a pause, Suzy's said more confidently, in a rush, 'There is one thing I am absolutely sure of, and that is that whoever is the cause, he is determined to get someone. The way the words came out, it sounded to me like he had been waiting and was now happy because the time had come to do whatever he planned to do, perhaps revenge.' She stopped for a moment to get her breath.

'I think you need to set some new rules,' Suzy continued. 'You need to make sure that you watch out for each other every day and make sure you know what everyone is doing where they are going. Then, you'll know that the source of the voice isn't anybody in your warren. Like Grandad says, it's easier to rule out who isn't doing things wrong, to find the culprit by elimination. I think that strategy might be helpful in this case. But whatever you decide to do, and whatever happens, I'm with you.'

Chamali thanked Suzy very much for her suggestions and said he was especially pleased to hear her talk so kindly about his people. He then thanked all the paxteys for coming and bid them farewell. He said he didn't doubt that there would be many meetings like this before the culprits were found. Then there was a loud droning noise and, *swish!* the visitors all set off in different directions for home.

Bira the albatross took off and headed out to sea to inform the King of the latest developments.

After the visiting paxteys had all gone, Chamali came over to Suzy and Scratch, who were standing with their friends Toomy and Tooby.

'You know,' Chamali said, 'I've realised that everyone here today said they only hear the voice in the mist, so I believe that the creature must need that mist to carry his voice. That isn't impossible, is it? After all, what do we do when we want to contact someone or send good feelings off to a creature or land far away?'

'We send the message on the air!' Scratch, Toomy, and Tooby said all at once.

'Exactly' Chamali responded. 'So we will be prepared the next time it is misty. If we follow the sound through the mist, and if we're fast enough, then maybe, just maybe, we can catch the source of the voice. But it won't be easy; even paxteys can't travel at the speed of sound. They nearly can, but not quite.'

Suzy listened, fascinated. This was going to be an adventure!

'What about my little house? Will it be able to keep up?'

'Your little house can go at the same speed as a paxtey,' Scratch said. 'After all, a paxtey taught it to fly.

'Tut-tut!' Chamali said rather impatiently. 'We can discuss how the little house flies later.'

Chamali, Scratch, and Suzy spent the next couple of hours discussing the Plan for the voice: All the adult paxteys would be on mist alert, and at the first scent of mist, All the adult Paxteys would gather above the

Warren, and when they heard the voice, they would follow it, no matter how far they had to go, to find its source. Suzy hoped that it wouldn't happen while she was at school, as she didn't want to miss it.

It was now very late in the evening, and she really needed to get home, as Julie would call for her tomorrow and they would go shopping. Suddenly the trip didn't seem important, but she knew she had to keep her normal life going as well so that nobody would follow her out of curiosity and stumble onto the little people and their homes.

Suzy wondered how she would know when the alarm had been raised, as she might not be around to hear it, but Chamali assured her that if she was at home she would know and that she wasn't to worry. He then thanked her for her time and wished her goodnight.

One more surprise awaited Suzy when she got back home: Julie had rung while she was out to say she was really worried because she, too, had heard the voice and thought it might have been someone calling out in the lane.

How was that possible? Suzy and her grandparents were puzzled, but they thought that maybe the paxteys had meant to choose her like they chose Suzy but had overlooked her.

Suzy, Nan, and Grandad decided to discuss it with Chamali as soon as possible.

Chapter 9

The Conchifleur

Julie was ready and waiting for Suzy at the end of the lane at 10.30 a.m. on the dot.

It was a bright, calm morning. *There's certainly no sign of mist*, Suzy thought.

'Hiya, Ju!' she called. They walked to the bus stop together, Julie chattering away about how she'd spend her money. She mentioned hearing the voice but didn't seem to think of it as anything serious, so Suzy thought it was best to leave it for now until she had a chance to talk about her knowledge of it with Scratch and Chamali.

Suzy thought the morning was never going to come to an end, although she had always loved the shops before, especially looking through all the CDs and DVDs. There was so much to think and care about with the Paxtey's that it was hard for her to concentrate. They strolled around the girly shops and tried on some smashing shoes with a big clumsy heel.

'I'm getting these!' Julie said excitedly. 'Wait till they see me down the club; they'll all want them!'

Suzy smiled in agreement.

'Oh, Su, you *must* come next week. It's *such* fun!' Julie said as they stood in the queue to pay.

'Well, I'll see if I get time. Really, I will.' Suzy said.

'What do you mean, if you get time? What is it, Su? Won't your Nan let you come?'

'It's not my Nan; she likes me to join in with things,' Suzy explained carefully.

'Then why can't you come?'

'Let's go and get a Pepsi or something,' Suzy said to change the subject. When they were through the checkout, she headed off for the coffee shop in the precinct with Julie close on her heels. They didn't say another word till they sat down with their Pepsis and chocolate éclairs.

Julie looked gingerly at her best friend in the whole world. They had started school together at five years old and had shared every little disaster and secret with each other ever since, but now she gave Suzy a look that said she was behaving really strangely and wasn't any fun anymore. Suzy knew that if anyone else were acting this way, Julie wouldn't bother with her.

'Su, I'm really worried about you. I know there's something wrong and I want to help if I can. Can't you tell me what it is?'

'Nothing is wrong,' Suzy replied, exaggerating the happiness in her voice. 'Why would you think something's wrong? I've just been busy, that's all. Honestly, Ju, there's nothing wrong, Now let's get on with our smashing éclair eh?'

Julie banged the table 'Busy with what?' she said, really agitated now.

'I'm sorry, but I can't tell you,' Suzy said.

'I thought you were supposed to be my best friend! Haven't we always shared all our secrets? Are you telling me that you can't trust me with whatever it is?'

'I am only saying that this is something I can't tell you about now. I'm really sorry. Please, Ju, don't ask me again. I just cannot tell you.'

They ate their éclairs in silence, and then went home on the bus in silence. They walked along the cliff road in silence. Suzy knew she would have to say something; she knew Julie was really hurt. Suzy stopped walking and turned to Julie.

'I'm really sorry. I don't want to upset you or hurt you, but—'

'It's too late for that! You already have,' Julie snapped.

'Well . . . I'm sorry. I don't want us to fall out and stuff, and you're right, something has happened in the last few months, something that I've got caught up in. But I've made a promise, you see. I've promised not to tell people about it.'

'It's a boy, isn't it? You've met a boy and you don't want to share the information with me, do you?' Julie wasn't going to be calmed down very easily.

'No! It's *not* a boy!' Suzy squealed. 'If it was, I'd tell you about him and this wouldn't be so difficult.'

'Well, what, is it then, eh? What is it?'

'I can't tell you; I really can't. I really have promised,' Suzy said quietly, hanging her head.

'Will you ever be able to tell me?' Julie said, softening, as if she would settle for any information.

'I hope so. I promise, I will tell you as soon as I can.' Suzy smiled at her friend, and they linked arms and continued their walk along the cliff path. Suzy was so relieved that that little squabble was over and she and Julie were okay again. They arranged to meet at the Clifftop Café Sunday morning—tomorrow—and to meet up with a couple of girls from school.

They waved goodbye to each other at the top of the lane and went their separate ways. Suzy breathed a huge sigh of relief; that had been a difficult morning. She would have hated to fall out with her best friend, but she had responsibilities to Scratch and his friends, and at the moment, those were more important. She smiled and shook her head. For now things would have to stay as they were.

That evening, during dinner, Grandad told Suzy and Nan about a strange plant he had spotted on the cliff path as he walked home from gardening club. It was huge, with flowers the size of a giant sunflower, although they were octagonal instead of round. Grandad said he didn't remember seeing them on the cliff, or anywhere else, for that matter, before.

Suzy thought back to earlier in the day when she was walking home. She remembered noticing that something was different, but because of the difficult discussion she was having with Julie, it stayed in the back of her mind, but she said she would make a point of looking for it the next day.

On Sunday morning, Suzy met Julie at the end of the lane as usual. It was a lovely morning, so they were able to take the cliff path and chat nineteen to the dozen. Their relationship was back to normal. *Thank goodness*, thought Suzy.

'I hope it's not muddy along this footpath. I'm wearing my new shoes,' Julie said.

'Yes, I can see that. They look very nice,' Suzy muttered, not really taking any notice of Julie because she couldn't believe her eyes. There must have been hundreds, no, *thousands* of the strange flowers that Grandad had mentioned. They stretched along the cliff as far as the eye could see. Each flower was the size of a giant sunflower, as Grandad had said, and was mainly cream coloured, but inside the petals where they met the face of the flower were six triangles which looked as though someone had stitched them on with deep mauve thread.

'Oh, I knew it! I've got mud all over my shoes,' Julie continued. Su you're not listening to a word I'm saying.

'My God, Ju! Have you ever seen such beautiful flowers? There's so many!'

'Yes, very nice,' Julie said in a huff. 'I'm getting off this stupid cliff and going over on the road.'

'Please, this is important. Will you listen to me and forget your shoes for a moment!'

That got Julie's attention, and she humoured her friend and looked at the flowers.

'I don't remember seeing these before. Do you?'

'No, but then, we never really looked at plants together before, did we?' Suzy mumbled through clenched teeth.

'I guess not. But these are strange, and they kinda make you look at them, don't they?'

At that, they just stood there, taking in the full picture. The flowers grew along the cliff as far as the eye could see in clumps of twelve.

'Look at those marks on the flowers,' Julie said. 'Your right they really do look like someone's stitched them on, don't they?'

But Suzy wasn't looking at the plants anymore because straight ahead was a group of paxteys, including Scratch, hovering above a group of flowers. Suzy hoped they would be so engrossed with the plants that they wouldn't notice her.

She heard Scratch's voice in her head. *Don't worry; your friend won't be able to see us. We will fly past you, and we can talk about these plants later. Bye for now.*

Julie continued chatting away, and Suzy nodded and smiled. Scratch and the group whooshed past at incredible speed.

Julie shivered. 'Ooh! Someone just walked over my grave. A chill went right down my back!'

Marvellous, Suzy thought.

Later, at the Cliff top Café, Suzy sat with her friends at a table that looked along the cliff. Everyone at the other tables was talking about the flowers, and some were taking pictures and videos of them.

If everyone can see them, then that means this isn't just a paxtey thing, Suzy thought. *But I can't help feeling that something is wrong. I know all these people are thinking this is really wonderful, but I've got a gut feeling that it's not.* Suzy often got that apprehensive feeling in the pit of her stomach when something wasn't right, and that's how she felt now.

At lunchtime, she left her friends and made her way home for Sunday lunch. When she was out of sight of her friends, Scratch appeared by her right shoulder.

'Hello,' he said. 'Have you had a nice time with your friends?'

'Yes. I'm sorry I wasn't here this morning.'

'Life must go on as usual, both for you and for me. You mustn't worry.'

'So what are these beautiful plants, Scratch?'

'Chamali says they haven't been seen since he was a young paxtey nearly 150 years ago. They are called conchifleurs. The strangest thing about them this time is that they have grown four times larger than they did the last time, and have you noticed that they have changed colour as the day has worn on?'

'Have they? How?' Suzy asked.

'Look at the dark marks towards the centre.'

'Yes, I see. The areas that look like mauve embroidery look thicker, as if the colour's bleeding. Oh, and look at that! The flowers' centres are starting to puff out, as though they're going to burst. I don't think I like the look of them now, Scratch! They also have a very peculiar smell.'

'I have to admit I'm very wary,' Scratch said with a puzzled look. 'These are definitely very strange flowers.'

Just before dark that evening, everyone but Grandad had disappeared off home and all was quiet along the cliff path—no one was even walking a dog. All the birds had gone to roost, and not a rabbit was in sight.

It was very quiet indeed; eerily quiet.

Clouds gathered fast. The evening sun had gone down over the horizon, and a gentle breeze blew through the trees and the grasses.

'Looks like we're in for some rain,' Grandad said, looking down on the warren from the cliff path. 'Good thing, really, we need it.'

Down in the warren, the paxteys thought differently and had hidden the paxtey babies and the other young ones safely away and had taken to the air. They hovered in silence, some along the cliff edge facing the plants, some above the trees, and some facing the sea, all listening to the wind.

Something was wrong. Something was coming. All their senses told them to watch, look, listen.

'Look at the conchifleurs! Look, look!' someone shouted.

The flowers were moving, very slowly raising their heads to the sky, towards the clouds, the wind, and the sea.

All the paxteys watched, their senses alert for something bad. Some of them were hovering in front of the conchifleurs in case anything got out of hand.

The flower heads continued to rise up, and then . . . nothing. The paxteys waited ten minutes, twenty minutes, and thirty minutes . . . an hour. The sky above grew darker and the clouds grew thicker and thicker. A storm rumbled in the distance. Lightning flashed across the sky.

Pargh!

The faces of the conchifleurs burst open, and all the paxteys nearby jumped back a few feet. Then, softly, something wailed, and it grew louder and louder.

Most of the paxteys flew into formation along the cliff, face-to-face with the flowers. Even though their faces were much smaller than the flowers', the paxteys were so brave and strong.

The wailing stopped and a crackling sound began as waves of energy, in orange flecked with red, flowed from the flowers to the clouds. The waves built and then connected and punctured the clouds with a sound as if a bomb had exploded. The paxteys tried to stop the waves by creating rainbow circles around them, but there weren't enough of them, they tried so hard, but this was beyond their capabilities. They were gentle, caring souls, not fighters.

Lightning flashed, thunder crashed, rain rushed down, and the wind became a gale, as the water ran down the cliff, the paxteys were washed down the steep cliffs along with the muddy water, with the loosened plants and bushes. Their little wings couldn't fight the storm to save themselves.

The paxteys that had been nearest the trees were hanging on to the thickest branches as tightly as they could. The young ones screamed as their dwellings filled with water, and the nurses snatched up the babies and hovered high up near the ceiling of the nursery to keep away from the water, which was rising fast. Their only way out was the skylight. Outside, trees fell.

The seawater had managed to run over into the warren, as the tide was very high, higher than had ever been known, and the sea defences couldn't keep it out. Not a single living creature—not a plant, a tree, or a paxtey—was safe.

Chamali had been sitting high up in a great oak tree observing his surroundings through a doorway in the big old trunk and had decided to go out onto the longest and highest branch to see what was happening when the storm hit, as, like all the older paxteys, he wanted to be ready when the time came.

That time never came for Chamali. The first massive fork of lightning flashed and hit the branch that he was standing on. He was caught by surprise, and his wings got stuck among the leaves, and he crashed forty feet to the ground. He lay in the mud, the rain pounding him, trying to collect his senses. A few moments were all he had.

Ogystone's faithful servants, Kurr and Kree, and some of his other slaves had been waiting for this moment. They pounced on Chamali, who tried hard to fight them off and shouted, but the sound of the storm drowned out his calls. They smothered him and wrapped him in a filthy cloth, gathering it at the top so he couldn't escape, and lifted him into the air, in seconds, they were gone.

Everyone was too busy trying to help each other, the young ones, and the animals, to stay out of the way of falling trees, and to keep out of the water and mud to notice what had happened to Chamali.

The first part of Ogystone's ugly plan had worked. His conchifleurs, his invention, had worked. 'With just a little tweak of nature,' he said, 'not all flowers are nice, are they?'

CHAPTER 10

The Lodgers

As he walked back along the cliff road, Grandad had seen the storm gathering and the paxteys, including Scratch, hovering watchfully, silently.

Go home, Grandad. Quickly, Scratch said in his head.

Grandad had that feeling in the pit of his stomach that something terrible was about to happen, that he should run and hide, and the hair on the back of his neck stood on end. But the paxteys didn't run and hide and neither did Grandad. He walked quickly and proudly back home.

As soon as he arrived, he found Nan in the kitchen. 'Where's Suzy?' he asked.

'She's in the garden.' Nan didn't ask questions; she knew Grandad was worried.

Suzy emerged from the little house when Grandad called her. She ran up the path. 'Can you feel it? The air is all on edge!'

'That's one way to describe it,' Grandad replied. 'We're certainly in for a bad storm.'

As soon as he knew, everyone was safely indoors, including the cat, Grandad sat by the kitchen window watching the sky. The clouds were gathering unusually fast now. He couldn't sit still, and he walked to the back door, with Suzy close behind. They stood out in the garden looking towards the cliffs. The clouds were now thick and black, and the sky was dark, like night had come early.

There was complete stillness and silence. Then a sound what was it? It was wailing and grinding.

Lightning flashed and thunder rumbled all around, and then there was one terrifying crash.

'That sounded like an explosion!' Grandad shouted. He pushed Suzy indoors and slammed the door just as extraordinarily heavy rain started.

The rain was so heavy that Suzy couldn't see through it as she, Nan, and Grandad watched through the window, and they couldn't hear each other speak. It seemed as if millions of stones had been thrown by the wind, which had reached gale force, into the house.

'Oh, Scratch, I hope you and your friends are safe. Please let them be safe,' Suzy whispered.

Crash! A window smashed upstairs.

'There goes that little window. I knew I should have had it glazed when I had the others done!' Grandad shouted above the noise. He went to the cupboard under the stairs and grabbed a hammer, nails, and a piece of wood that he Nan and Suzy built jigsaw puzzles on and ran upstairs to cover the window.

Suzy sat with Nan. *Poor Nan,* Suzy thought. *She hates thunderstorms.* 'You okay, Nan? Shall I put the kettle on?'

'Good idea, love. I'm okay. We're safe here, aren't we?'

'We'll be fine.'

After an hour, the storm finally stopped, as suddenly as it had started. From every window all Suzy could see was water. The drains hadn't been able to take the deluge, and every nook and cranny in the ground had been filled with water. The lawn looked like a lake, with the pond in it somewhere. The potted palms lay on the ground broken, and the guttering hung off the shed. Everywhere Suzy looked were tree branches and broken plants floating in the water. Two of the large trees in the lane had crashed down on the borders of the garden, and—

'Oh no!' Suzy shrieked. The little house had fallen over into the water.

She and Grandad waded through the water to rescue the little house. Together they heaved it back up onto its base and saw that it was fine; it had sustained just a little bit of damage to the decorative part of the window frame.

'Don't worry about that,' Grandad said. 'I can fix it later.' He smiled.

Suzy was so relieved that her mode of transport was okay, as she was anxious to see if Scratch and the other paxteys were all right.

'Grandad, I've got to go down to the warren. Do you think the storm is really over now?'

'I think you'll be okay, but perhaps you should stay in hovering mode in the little house. I don't think you should try to land. I'm going to get back to Nan, as there's nothing I can do out here till this water has subsided.'

Suzy went into the little house. 'Away, to the warren to find Scratch!' she shouted, wondering if the fall may have stopped it from flying. There was no need to worry.

Whoosh! The little house took off and was in the warren in a flash. As it slowly hovered along the tops of the trees, Suzy was horrified at what she saw. She couldn't have landed if she had wanted to, for the warren was like a swamp, and a mudslide had come down the cliffs from just above the dwellings. Fortunately the paxteys had a special texture on their wings, which kept the mud from sucking them down, and many of them had been able to fly out of danger. The young ones and the Paxtey babies however were terrified, and the community's dwellings had all been flooded.

Suzy surveyed the scene through the doorway as she slowly moved across the warren. Paxteys darted from tree to tree rescuing animals and even birds that had fallen into the mud. She couldn't see Scratch.

'Where is he?' she whispered to herself. A puff of strong warm air blew across her face, and there he was.

'Oh, Scratch, thank goodness! What a storm. Just look at the state of this place. What will you do? There's water everywhere, and windows smashed. We all jumped at the noise, and little house blew over. Oh, I'm so glad you're all right. You are all right, aren't you?' She hugged Scratch and big tears ran down her face.

'When I can speak I'll tell you!' Scratch gasped.

'Sorry! I'm so sorry.' Suzy sniffed, she put him down, and wiped her eyes.

'Right now, I'm fine,' Scratch said. 'We have much work to do and many creatures to rescue, but at the moment, the young ones and the babies are our top priority, for the nurseries are all underwater. We have to find somewhere safe and dry for them'.

'Well, there's only one thing for it. They'll have to stay in our house,' Suzy suggested. 'I'll go and talk to Nan and Grandad and tell them what's happening. Can I take the young ones back in the little house?'

'No, they'll come to you as soon as I can get them all together,' Scratch replied. 'But you could take some of their things with you.'

Suzy followed Scratch further into the warren to a spot high on a boulder out of the water that one of the paxtey nurses had found. All the cribs for the little ones, with their feeders and the other things they needed, had already been set up. Suzy helped them load it all into the little house, and then Scratch went to explain to everyone where they were going.

Suzy and the little house whooshed back to the garden.

'Nan, Grandad!' she shouted as she ran to the house, her feet splashing and squelching in the water and mud. 'The paxteys need help!' she called as she took off her boots.

Nan and Grandad looked up from their cups of tea.

'It's terrible!' Suzy went on. 'They've been washed out, and there's nowhere for the young ones to go till the other paxteys fix them up with somewhere dry, and I told them that you would help. I'm sorry to dump this on you, but you will help, won't you?'

'Of course we will,' Nan and Grandad answered in unison.

'I know the very thing we'll need,' Grandad said. 'You two clear the sitting room floor as much as you can. I'm going to the garage.'

They used the sitting room only on special occasions, and this was certainly a special occasion. Suzy and Nan moved the sofa and armchairs to the wall and moved everything else to the spare room. Then Scratch appeared in the kitchen.

'It's all right!' Suzy said. 'Nan and Grandad said it's okay. Grandad's gone to the garage to get something, but I don't know what it is.'

'I've seen him,' Scratch said. 'The babies will be here any minute.'

Grandad came back from the garage with two huge rolled-up tent bags, and right behind him came the nurses with the tiny babies in their arms. Nan ushered them into the kitchen, and the nurses stood on the kitchen table looking sad and tired.

Grandad busied himself setting up in the sitting room. He'd remembered that he had two tents that he used for fishing, which looked a bit like igloos, that would be ideal for the babies and their nurses, and he thought the sofa and armchairs would be comfy for all the other young ones. It wasn't long before, he came to the kitchen doorway.

'Right then. If you would all follow me, please, we will get you comfortable.' The nurses flew into the sitting room behind Grandad. Scratch, Nan and Suzy followed, carrying all the belongings Suzy had brought over in the little house, and Scratch passed them into the tents. The nurses got the cribs set up inside the tents, and Suzy heard tiny little whimpers and cries as the nurses settled the babies down.

Scratch then dashed off to fetch the next lot of young ones, and when he returned with several youngsters and their helpers, oh, dear, this was a whole different story. These youngsters were nervous, as they hadn't left the warren before, and all these big humans and the house were just too frightening. They took turns crying, and even the bravest of them, even one who usually stayed silent, cried. The trauma of the storm had been bad enough, and being taken away from their home was too much.

Nan and Suzy went into the sitting room with them, covered the floor of the second tent with cushions, and snuggled the frightened young ones into the cushions. Their carers gave them some elderberry juice to drink and berries to eat. Soon all was quiet.

Suzy felt quite pleased that she, Nan, and Grandad had been able to help.

'The paxteys are so sweet,' Nan said to Grandad with a smile. 'And all those little ones! I had forgotten how tiny they are.'

Grandad nodded and smiled too, but he said his mind was on more practical matters, for he planned to go down to the warren in the morning to see if he could do anything to help.

Meanwhile, back in the warren, all the paxteys were working hard to return everything to normal, if that were possible, and checking on each other now that the little ones were safe. Scratch had returned, and they all met in the clearing where the paxtey haven had been held, but now it was underwater. They hovered in a group over the clearing and discussed the damage

Worse news was too come: six paxteys were missing, one of whom was Chamali. A group went to find him first, having seen that his tall oak tree had lost one of the large branches where he could usually be seen munching on a long stem of rye grass on nice evenings. The paxteys of the warren had been expecting him to take charge and lead them like he always did, but there was no sign of him.

They worked long into the night, clearing the mess, but they couldn't find any of the missing paxteys.

'They couldn't have puffed out, could they?' Scratch asked.

'No, they are all far too young for that,' Skeet answered.

Finally, after searching everywhere and questioning everyone, Scratch and the other paxteys had to accept the horrible truth: Chamali had gone, and five of their friends had gone with him. Some thought that maybe Chamali had been so devastated because he hadn't been able to keep his group safe that he may have puffed out due to shame. Others didn't believe it and carried on searching. Chamali was too strong, too determined to puff out. He would have wanted to see this disaster through, they said.

The remaining paxteys searched for Chamali and the five other missing paxteys for days asked everyone they saw about their whereabouts, but no one had seen them; they had all been too busy helping each other. They also questioned all the animals in and around the warren, and all had a tale to tell. The rabbits' tales were probably the saddest because every little family had lost someone, as many of their burrows had been flooded. The hedgehogs hadn't been able to get to safety, either, and the same was true of the moles, voles, and mice. Hundreds had been buried or drowned on that terrible day.

A vixen had been running for higher ground to get her three cubs to safety, and she had managed to get two cubs onto a stone ledge away from the water, but when she went back for her third cub, she got caught in a mudslide, and she and her cub had been buried in the mud. The paxteys found the two cubs who had survived sitting on the ledge crying for their mother and took them off to another vixen in the warren that was pining for her four lost cubs.

Towards the end of the day, Scratch and the others had just one area that they hadn't checked, the pond. It had escaped any damage because the rocks all around it had sheltered it from the storm, and just a few leaves and twigs floated on the surface. Its occupants had been able to watch everything that went on in the warren, and they had seen what had happened to Chamali.

Scratch sat on Chamali's storytelling rock. The warren was so quiet now that there were no little ones running around, giggling, and chasing each other. Ten days had passed since that terrible night, and the babies were still with Suzy. It was taking much longer than any of the paxteys thought to make the warren safe enough for them to come back.

Scratch wondered, pondered, and considered as he sat.

'Chamali didn't puff out; I just know he didn't. He's alive somewhere, I can feel it.' Scratch even considered the possibility that Chamali may have tried to follow the source of the storm down the wind and had somehow got lost or couldn't get back. As he thought deeply, he became aware of a slap, slap, slap.

Scratch turned towards the water and saw, to his surprise, several fish slapping the surface of the water in order to communicate with him. For most creatures, to converse with fish was impossible, but paxteys were able to speak with fish just as easily as speaking with each other because of a natural connection with nature and the spirit of the earth itself. They were gifted with the power of a special telepathy for all creatures and people.

The perch and the sticklebacks jostled for the top position in the pond, and as their mouths opened and closed, sending bubbles to the surface, Scratch was able to understand what they were saying. They had seen Kurr and Kree, paxteys that looked like rocks, and some smaller paxteys the same size as Scratch who looked puffed out but wasn't, gather up the other five. Chamali had tried to fight them off, even though he was outnumbered. Scratch felt proud of Chamali and so relieved to know that he and the others hadn't puffed out. He thanked the fish and apologised to them for not listening to them sooner.

Just as he was about to leave, he heard a rush of wings and the familiar squeak of a bat. It was Chamali's pet bat, Peeps. It flew straight towards him and landed on his shoulder, and the tale he told Scratch was even more amazing than the one the fish had just told him. It was enough to convince him; he knew what he had to do.

He then went off to tell the other paxteys what the bat had told him, and then he went to speak to Suzy and her grandparents. It was time for him and Suzy to find King Tobias.

Chapter 11

Chamali the Hostage

Everything had happened so quickly for Chamali: One moment he was trying to recover from the shock of falling out of his tree, and the next strange paxteys had pounced on him. He had been winded in the fall and all his energy had disappeared, so he couldn't fight them off. They had bundled him into a bag, and he was flying through the air, but where?

Who are these paxteys, if indeed that's what they are? He thought.

They looked so odd. They had no colour and were almost ghostly, and those two big, fat ones? All covered in lumps. They looked like paxteys turned to stone.

How did they get to be like that? Chamali wondered. In all his years, he had never seen paxteys like them!

He bumped and swung along in the air until he felt himself descending. The air was very cold now, and it was still pitch black even though Chamali felt that it should be dawn.

Bump! Chamali hit the ground with a mighty thud. 'Oomph!' he gasped.

Then a voiced boomed through the air, 'Over here! Bring him over here!'

I know that voice, Chamali thought to himself as he was roughly dragged across the floor.

'Here! At my feet!'

It was the voice from the mist!

Rough hands opened the sack, and a foot gave Chamali a swift kick, and he rolled flat on his face across the cold stone ground.

He stopped at Ogystone's feet.

Oh, I'm too old for this! He thought as he tried to visualise his lovely moss-covered stone back home and the young ones sitting around it waiting for their story. He lay as still as possible, trying to get his wind back. Slowly, he opened his eyes and looked to his right. Just a couple of inches away from his face were two rather fat and bumpy grey-and-brown feet with toenails full of dirt. He shifted onto his side, and his eyes scanned upwards. Attached to the feet were fat warty legs followed by a large body covered in sackcloth.

Ogystone was taller than Chamali had expected, and he was so fat that he looked as wide as he was tall. Every bit of his grey-brown flesh was covered in warts. Chamali couldn't see his neck; Ogystone's head just seemed to sit on his shoulders. Small clumps of spiky hair with bald spots in between poked out of the top of his head.

Chamali slowly shifted himself into a sitting position as he stared at the hideous smile on Ogystone's gloating face.

'Welcome to your new home!' Ogystone boomed.

Chamali stared into his face. When Ogystone spoke, his lips hardly moved. In all Chamali's nearly two hundred years, he really had never seen anything or anyone that looked so monstrously ugly and horrifying.

'Who are you? Chamali groaned when he finally managed to sit on one of his many bruises. 'What is this place?'

Ogystone looked over at Kurr and Kree, who were sitting nearby looking very pleased with themselves. He then looked back at Chamali. Ogystone's eyes held a glint of hatred as he spat the answer. 'This place is where you will spend whatever is left of your miserable little life. I will have the pleasure of watching you *sufferrrrr*! Huh!'

Chamali looked around him and saw only rock, dirt, and hard ground. These creatures, whatever they were, blended in with the scenery. There was something special about that big one; he was obviously the leader. Chamali reasoned that the others were his servants, and they seemed very eager to please him. He had such a strong feeling that he knew that big one from long ago, but from where?

Chamali licked his parched lips, but he was so thirsty and his mouth was so dry that his tongue had no moisture.

Ogystone banged the arm of his stone seat with what looked like a ladle made from bone. 'Bring some refreshments for our guest!' he shouted.

Within seconds, a paxtey slowly flew across towards Chamali, who could not believe his eyes. This was unlike any paxtey he had ever seen: his glow had disappeared, and all that was left was a dusty, sad, grey face topped with grubby hair. In place of a special garment, he wore a lifeless, colourless cloth that looked like netting.

Chamali took water from him but refused the strange food which was offered that looked like mashed-up pond weed. As Chamali put the drink to his lips, he looked into the eyes of the paxtey before him

'Oh my word!' he gasped. It was Karolle, a paxtey who had vanished in last year's storms. Everyone in the warren thought he had puffed out. The light in his eyes had gone, and just black pupils stared back at him.

'Karolle, is that you? Are you all right?' *What a stupid question,* Chamali thought as soon he had said those words. *Of course he isn't all right.*

Karolle didn't answer. His paxtey spirit was gone, and he seemed totally unaware that Chamali was even there his only thought was to serve his master, to do as he was told. Then he would be given that lovely plant for his meal later on, and everything would be fine.

Chamali was so shocked that he turned to Ogystone and shouted, 'What have you done to him? Why has he lost his light?' He was so angry he had completely forgotten where he was and the danger he was in.

Ogystone picked up the bone ladle and rushed across the floor. With one mighty swoop, he hit Chamali across the shoulder, knocking the drink from Chamali's hand and sending him to the floor. Then Ogystone roared, 'You will never raise your voice to me in that manner, *again*! You will never question anything I do, *ever*! The condition of my men is of *no* concern of yours!'

With each angry sentence, Ogystone stamped on Chamali, who groaned.

'You are here now to serve me and do as you are told! You will not trouble yourself anymore, because soon you will be just like my men— you won't care. Har har harrr!' Ogystone stood there and smiled a smile of deep satisfaction, as though he hadn't enjoyed himself this much for years.

'Now, do you still want to know who I am?'

Chamali could only nod; he was in too much pain to speak. Besides, he finally recognised Ogystone once he had started shouting. This monster had been just like him many, many years before; they had shared the same home. Chamali planned to see what this was all about before he did anything.

'I will tell you who I am, and then you will tell me everything I want to know,' Ogystone said, pleasantly now. 'Now that's fair, isn't it?'

Chamali glared back at him as he thought about what to say next. He was very sore thanks to those warty feet and so tired. Even so, he was determined that he would never bow to Ogystone's commands. After all, he was Chamali, leader of the Capel paxteys! He watched Karolle slowly leaving the cavern through an archway to his left, and he also noticed other paxteys hovering dismally, looking dark and forlorn, at the other end of the cavern.

Ogystone watched Chamali and waited for his answer. 'Those men over there are waiting for their master to give them a command. They love to serve me; they are totally devoted to me.'

Chamali slowly rose from the ground so he could look Ogystone in the face. He looked around once more. The paxteys at the back of the room all bent their heads and averted their eyes as though they were fearful Chamali would see the bad things they had done, but he knew those things weren't their fault; their evil master had stolen their spirits. Just how Chamali didn't know, but he was determined to find out.

'Now listen to me, whoever you are,' Chamali said forcefully to Ogystone through clenched teeth. He was in terrible pain but would never show it. 'I will never bow to your command. I will never tell you anything if it doesn't suit me to tell you. And I most certainly will never become like them.' He waved his hands towards the paxteys behind him. 'If you think I will, then—' Crack! Swish! Swish! Chamali screamed as Kurr and Kree hit him with long bone poles.

'Get him; get him!' Ogystone screamed.

Chamali crashed to the floor. It was hopeless. He couldn't fight those two.

'Harder, harder!' Ogystone shouted.

As the blows rained down on Chamali, he decided he would rather puff out than give in to the evil around him. Then, suddenly, he remembered he did have a defence. The rainbow shield!

He muttered, 'Rainbow, rainbow, around me. Rainbow, oh rainbow. Where are you, rainbow?' For a moment, Chamali thought the shield wouldn't come, that this terrible rock cavern may stop anything good from happening, but finally he saw it. Yes! It was that wonderful, luminous rainbow glow.

Biff! Biff! Biff! The bone poles couldn't touch him now as Chamali concentrated on his rainbow shield. The others couldn't see it and seemed not to understand what was happening. Whatever happened now, Chamali would stay inside his shield and stay safe.

Ogystone stamped and screeched. Then, suddenly, he sat down, exhausted. 'Leave him. Let me think!'

He sat still for what seemed like hours, thinking of a way to penetrate that shield. Then, he waved to the paxteys at the back of the cavern. 'Get over here!'

Chamali sat and rubbed his wounds and tried to straighten his wings, wondering what was coming next.

Several paxteys hovered around Chamali, not daring to look at him and waiting to be told what to do.

'Kurr and Kree, escort our guest to his room,' Ogystone ordered. 'We will have another little chat later.'

Kurr signalled to a small group cowering against a wall to pick Chamali up, and they did despite his rainbow shield, and marched him off in a procession past Ogystone. If Chamali hadn't been in so much pain he would have waved. Thank goodness he had remembered his rainbow. He was sure he would have puffed out without it.

Under the archway they went out into a dimly lit corridor, and they seemed to travel along this corridor for a very long time. From the colour of the rock all around, Chamali had realised that they were a long way underground some time ago. And what was that smell? At first it was the damp, musky smell that he expected to smell underground, but now, what was that? It smelled sweet and pungent, and though it was not unpleasant, Chamali knew it wasn't good.

Suddenly the paxteys carrying him stopped in front of a door with a grille. Kurr opened it and stood back, and so did Kree. They waved the other paxteys inside.

'Drop him over there,' Kree said. The others did exactly as they were told, but thanks to the rainbow shield, Chamali didn't drop but floated gently to the ground. Kurr and Kree looked disgusted that he hadn't crashed to the floor in terrible pain.

'You'll find plenty of food and drink here. Help yourself. I do hope you will be comfortable!' Kurr called out sarcastically as he led the other paxteys out.

One little paxtey hung back, Chamali noticed that he wasn't as dark and dusty as the others. He said quickly and silently, in Chamali's mind, *Sir; please do not eat the green weed. It is very dangerous.*

Then this paxtey left, too, and the door slammed behind him. Chamali was alone at last. He looked around and saw that this wasn't just a room, it was a prison cell. It was dark, smelly, and damp. A glow at the back from luminous stones gave him some light, and he saw food and water. He decided to just have the water. He wondered what that young paxtey had meant by his warning not to eat the weed, for it smelled very nice and looked very fresh.

Just like the weedy grass we have at home, he thought. Then Chamali noticed an after smell that wafted to his nose sneakily. *He's right; this is dangerous. All my instincts are saying not to eat it. So this is what has changed them, what has stolen their light and taken away their personalities and their care. I must think. What to do, what to do?*

Chamali sat down and gathered his cosy rainbow bubble around him to think. He had to find a way to get out or to send a message home.

But how?

Two days passed in which he didn't see or hear anyone. In spite of his nasty, dark, damp surroundings, his bumps and bruises were nearly healed, and a crack in his wing had knitted together. Early in the morning of the third day, he heard the other paxteys. They were coming to get him.

What will happen now? Fear welled up in his tummy, and his rainbow bubble faded.

'No, don't leave me,' he whispered. 'I need you now. Please stay.' He took a deep breath and visualised the rainbow shield, wishing it back. 'Oh, thank goodness.' He sighed with relief as the warmth around him returned. He knew that no matter what happened, he could not let the fear come back, he could not allow any negative thoughts in, and he had to be strong.

He took another deep breath and stood up straight. 'Just you remember who you are: Chamali, leader of the Capel paxteys,' he said loudly and so proudly that the Rainbow sphere around him became even stronger.

Thud! The door burst open to reveal Kurr and Kree and their band of pitiful helpers.

'Your presence is requested at breakfast with our master,' they said in unison. Kurr and Kree signalled to the others to pick Chamali up and carry him off along the musty passages. As they marched along, Chamali communicated by thought with the paxtey closest to him.

What is your name? Where do you come from?

He received no response.

It must be too late for him, Chamali thought with a sad sigh.

They entered the big cavern where Chamali had first been taken, and there was Ogystone on a stone seat at a table, smiling unpleasantly.

'Aha! Good morning to you, Chamali! So good of you to join me for the first morning meal.

'I'm very pleased to see you have regained your composure this morning, sir,' Chamali replied with an exaggerated bow.

'And do I assume from your respectful manner that your three-day incarceration has persuaded you to be co-operative?' boomed Ogystone sarcastically.

'You are mistaking good manners for subservience, sir,' Chamali replied sweetly.

Ogystone's expression changed to anger instantly, showing that he had finally accepted that he wouldn't get his way through torture or oppression. This paxtey was far too clever for that.

'Sit!' he commanded. 'We shall eat!'

Chamali sat opposite him. On the table were what appeared to be berries and grasses and juice, but his senses told him not to touch anything. He knew that things here were not what they appeared to be.

'So, Chamali, let's try to bridge the divide,' Ogystone said quietly. 'I don't want to be at war with you. After all, we were brothers once.' Ogystone's voice was quiet now. He stopped to allow the shock of his disclosure to sink in.

Chamali was indeed shocked. He had known that this creature was familiar to him, but he would never have believed that Ogystone, this abominable mistake of nature, could have once been his brother. However, he kept total control of his feelings and didn't allow his shock to show on his face.

'Well, Ogystone, *dear brother*,' Chamali replied, 'you really have come a long way since we last met over a century ago. You must be very proud of your kingdom of captives.'

'My kingdom of captives is very happy to be here. As I told you before, they live to serve me.'

'The way I see it, they serve you to live,' Chamali shot back.

'Enough!' Ogystone shouted. 'All I need now in order to complete my kingdom is my third brother. And how is good King Tobias?' Ogystone asked, straining to compose himself once again.

'His Majesty King Tobias is very well and very safe, and, I might add, he is doing a very gracious job.'

'I'm sure he is. I would like the opportunity to visit him. Perhaps after you have eaten you might like to tell me where I could find him.' Ogystone's smile was almost sickening.

It didn't fool Chamali. *I know exactly what you are up to,* he thought.

'You great sickening *maggot*!' Chamali yelled. 'Do you think I could be fooled into telling you where he is? Never will I tell you anything that would get him hurt!'

Chamali could almost feel the shocked silence around the cavern as everyone froze, waiting to see what was coming next.

Ogystone let out a terrible scream and turned a very deep maroon. 'Get him out, get him *out*! Lock him away forever! No food, no water! I want him *dead*!'

So that's the colour of rage, Chamali thought as everyone rushed forward to seize him and rush him out of the chamber. He was back in his cell in no time, with not a word said by Kurr or Kree. They dumped him, locked the door, sealed it, and that was that.

Well, Chamali thought. *This is it; this is where I will stay until I puff out.* He sat for a long time thinking over the things he had been told. How was it possible that he and Tobias could have had a brother like Ogystone? Nature must have made a mistake.

Are we somehow responsible? He thought with horror. *I'm so tired!*

He would sleep for now; his dreams would give him the answer. When he woke up, he would know what to do.

Chamali didn't sleep for long. He dreamt that he was sitting high up in his tree, the leaves rustling louder and louder in the wind. He awoke with a start as he realised the rustling was actually here in his cave. He was not alone. He frantically looked around. Who was it?

A tiny voice called, 'Chamali! Chamali, I'm up here!'

Chamali looked up at the ceiling. He couldn't see anything

'Over here, Chamali. I'm in the corner.'

Chamali picked up one of the luminous stones and held it up to the corner of the ceiling, and there, in the deepest crevice, was the sweet face of a tiny bat, his round eyes brightly reflecting the light of the stone. This was Chamali's pet bat, Peeps, who usually never left his side at the warren.

'At last I have found you! I followed your scent on the airwaves, but now I have found you, I am unable to get you out. What can I do? What has happened to you?'

'Oh, Peeps my dear friend! How I have missed you how nice to have someone from home with me!' Chamali said, taking the bat in his arms and hugging him gently. Tears ran down Chamali's cheeks.

They sat quietly together for a little while, and then Chamali had an idea.

'Listen, Peeps. I am going to give you a very responsible job.'

Peeps crawled onto Chamali's shoulder so he could listen properly.

'I want you to go back to the Warren, find Scratch, and tell him everything. Then, tell him to find King Tobias. He will know what to do.'

Peeps said he didn't want to leave Chamali alone, as he was frightened for him, but Chamali convinced him that he would be helping more if he went. As Peeps disappeared through a tiny hole in the ceiling, Chamali felt an immense sense of loss and loneliness. He wished his little friend a safe journey and hoped that somehow, someday, he would come back and bring someone who could help him.

Chapter 12

The Search Continues

Scratch went to the highest point of the cliff and flew back and forth until he found a south-westerly breeze heading towards northern France. Then, hovering on the spot, he concentrated really hard, just as Chamali had shown him, and sent his message:

'Very important to see King Tobias. I have news of Chamali.'

Not wanting to get in the way, Suzy decided to keep a safe distance in the little house and watch. She was intrigued. How could he know he had found the right spot from which to send the message? How would he know if the other paxteys had even received his message?

I wonder if I could send a message like that, she thought. For now, she waited with Scratch.

She wasn't quite sure exactly what they were waiting for, and she couldn't help having a quiet giggle to herself as she watched Scratch hovering several feet in the air, moving with the breeze, in a seated, crossed-legged position.

He looks like one of Nan's Buddha ornaments. She chuckled.

Then she remembered the heated discussion at the dinner table the night before. Nan had been really worried when Scratch had told them his plan.

'Suzy's going to go across the sea to the mountains of northern France in the little house.'

Nan shrieked in horror. 'Absolutely not! I'm sorry, Scratch, but I never realised Suzy's special role meant she was going to go to another country. I can't allow it. It's just not safe . . .' She hesitated. 'Is it?'

Nan looked at Grandad, who said visiting the King was a very good place to start.

Suzy felt her tummy twitch with excitement. 'Nan, please, if you give me permission, I might be able to visit the King's palace! Please, Nan!'

Finally Nan had agreed, and then it seemed only fair that Suzy should agree to her request to pack the little house with everything she could possibly need for every possible contingency, and she gave Nan no argument. They packed water and sandwiches, sweets and biscuits for Suzy, berry juice for Scratch, a first-aid box, and Suzy's shell jacket with a hood, an umbrella, and wellies.

Finally, Nan said, 'There's a duvet under the seat as well should you find you have to sleep, and Grandad has made a folding screen to cover the doorway and windows.'

'Ah, Nan, you really are the best! Thanks, Grandad.' Suzy hugged them both.

Her thoughts were jolted back to the present when she heard the sound they had been waiting for, something like static on a radio when you're trying to tune into a station. Scratch waved to Suzy and shouted, 'It's okay! They have received the message!'

Suzy moved closer to him. 'Now what do we do?'

'We wait,' Scratch responded.

They sat in little house together and stared out to sea watching, but for what they didn't know. It was a busy afternoon out there, as Suzy saw many ships in all shapes and sizes. She could just make out the land mass that was France; she knew that whatever was going to happen now, the instruction would come from over there. She watched the fishing boats and patrol boats heading into the harbour, flocks of gulls following in their wake, hoping for some good pickings from the fisherman as they cleaned and prepared their catch for market. She was surprised to see a large flock of pigeons flying in as well. *Probably racing pigeons*, she thought. There were also a group of large cormorants taking turns swooping and diving head first into the sea, more gulls, a couple of albatrosses, and . . . huh? Albatrosses!

'Scratch, look! Albatrosses are coming!' Suzy shouted as loudly as she could and pushed Scratch so hard he fell on the floor.

'Goodness me Suzy! Do you have to be so rough?'

'Oh, I'm sorry, Scratch.' She scooped him up and put him back on the seat. 'But look. I can see albatrosses heading this way.'

They went to the front of the little house and watched as the trio of albatrosses flew towards them. Many of the paxtey elders popped up around them; they had seen the birds coming, too.

Bira the largest albatross landed whilst the other two circled overhead, keeping watch. Scratch went to greet Bira, who bent his long neck and head in greeting.

'Good afternoon, Scratch.'

'I'm very pleased to see you,' Scratch said, bowing respectfully.

'His Majesty has asked me to escort you to his castle. If you would follow me, please we must leave immediately.'

'Yes, of course, thank you,' Scratch said with a nod. 'My friend Suzy will come, too, if she may.'

'As you wish. She will follow in that?' He nodded at the little house. Suzy was sure that she could see disbelief in his eyes, if it were possible for an albatross to show disbelief.

'Yes, this vessel is very worthy,' Scratch replied.

'Then we will go!' Bira screeched, and he took off from the cliff edge.

Scratch followed and called back to Suzy as he went, 'Tell the little house to follow!'

Suzy jumped back in, closed the gate, and pulled the bar down. 'Little house, away! Follow Scratch!' she called.

Within seconds, they were airborne and heading out to sea. Suzy looked back at the cliffs, which were way below her now. The paxtey elders that had come to welcome Bira were all waving them on their way and sending a clear message over the airwaves: *Keep safe, and be very careful!*

Even further back from the edge of the cliff, in her garden, Suzy saw Nan and Grandad waving furiously.

'Oh my lovely Nan and Grandad! I'll be back soon,' she whispered to herself with tears in her eyes. 'Come on girl, enough of that,' she told herself with a sigh. She then took a deep breath and looked ahead.

The three albatrosses led the way, followed by Scratch and then the little house as they headed across the channel toward the French coast. The water glistened and rippled below. As they got further out, Suzy saw a huge tanker below them.

Geez, she thought. *You could land a plane on that! It looks like a runway.*

Before long, they were over the coast of France.

I wonder where the King lives, she thought. *Will he live in a castle like a human king? I don't think he'll live in a little warren like the Capel paxteys. His house has to be something beautiful.*

They seemed to be flying for ages when, at last, they approached a huge mountain range and descended through some very dark clouds.

Hmm. Looks very stormy over here, Suzy thought.

Down, down they went, the little house following Scratch quite slowly into a giant crevice on the side of a mountain until they came to a halt on the ground.

Scratch popped his head in the doorway. 'Come on, Suzy! We have to follow Bira along this pathway.'

Suzy quickly jumped out and followed Scratch, taking a good look around as she went.

Suzy hadn't got much time to admire the view when something caught her eye: a seedling just starting to grow. She recognised it instantly, and the hair on the back of her neck pricked up, and was covered in goose pimples.

It was a conchifleur!

Scratch and Suzy called each other's names in unison.

'Oh no we must warn everyone!' Scratch said.

They hurried along the pathway, Suzy jogging along, trying to keep up with Scratch as he flew.

The pathway turned to the left, and suddenly, Suzy screeched, 'Wow!'

'How beautiful' Scratch said.

Before them was a sight to behold: nestling in a valley was the King's palace, surrounded by a paxtey hamlet. The palace looked as if it had been hewn out of the mountainside, and it was perfectly disguised. Nobody outside the paxtey world would have been able to see it. Suzy could see it, of course, as she was very much part of the paxtey world now. The palace glittered and sparkled in the late afternoon sun as if it were made of precious stones.

The storm clouds building up behind them urged them towards it.

Along the pathway was a small bridge that took them through an archway and into the castle. The two smaller albatrosses stopped at the bridge and stood guard whilst Bira continued across the bridge with Scratch and Suzy following. They passed under the ornamental archway into a large courtyard. The castle was enormous by paxtey standards, but, Suzy realised, it wasn't enormous by human standards. *It's not so much a castle as a beautiful French Chateau*, Suzy thought.

Four large towers gradually descended into the main building, which had many tiny windows, each reflecting that lovely rainbow glow that Suzy had come to know so well.

One doorway large enough for Suzy to walk through led into the main building, but if the rooms inside were tiny, it was quite possible that she would have to stay outside. Scratch looked back at her and seemed to know what she was thinking.

'If you wait here a moment, I'll go inside to see if the building is suitable for you.'

Suzy nodded and smiled; she was glad she hadn't had to say anything.

She estimated that the main part of the chateau was about a third of the size of Dover Castle. As Scratch went through the door, she was able to see a large hall that seemed to have a high ceiling.

In a few seconds, Scratch came back and beckoned her inside. They entered the main hall, where King Tobias was waiting for them. Suzy was really surprised, as she had imagined meeting the King would happen like it did in the movies: she would quietly approach the King who would be sitting on his throne, and, keeping her eyes cast down, she would curtsy humbly. But this wasn't like that at all.

King Tobias was sitting at a table on the far side of the hall speaking with a couple of officials, and when he saw them approach, he got up and came straight over to them. Scratch bowed and Suzy curtseyed, and as they rose, King Tobias reached forward and took their hands.

'My dear Scratch and Suzy, welcome. I am pleased you could come so quickly. If only it were under more pleasant circumstances. Sad, sad times. Poor Chamali.' He shook his head in despair.

'We are all feeling his loss, Your Majesty, Scratch said quietly, almost tearfully.

Suzy felt tears prickling her eyes, too. She took a deep breath and fought them back.

'Come. We will sit over here and talk,' King Tobias said.

Suzy and Scratch sat at the table with His Majesty and drank a flavoured drink that reminded Suzy very much of one of the herbal teas that Nan sometimes drank.

'Mmm, this is very nice,' she said.

'Yes, it is my favourite hot drink,' His Majesty said with a smile. 'It's made from a plant that grows on this very mountain.' He waved his hands toward the mountain with pride.

Suzy sat and quietly sipped her drink as Scratch explained in minute detail everything that had happened at the Capel warren. When he mentioned that Suzy's grandparents had allowed all the young ones and the babies and their nurses to stay in their house, the King smiled at Suzy and said, 'I must personally thank them as soon as I possibly can.'

Scratch went on to tell His Majesty about Chamali's pet bat.

'Will his pet be able to lead us to Chamali?' His Majesty asked.

'Yes,' Scratch said, 'but rescuing him will be very dangerous. Peeps is tiny and able to evade detection over the airwaves, but going to where Chamali is, to the Isle of Misty Fear is controlled by a terrible monster called Ogystone.'

'Ugh!' The King coughed and spluttered.

Suzy thought his drink had gone down the wrong way, but then the King took a deep breath and gathered himself.

'Ogystone!' he shouted, looking at Scratch. 'You did say *Ogystone*, correct?'

'Y-yes,' Scratch stuttered. 'Have I said something wrong?'

'Oh, no, Scratch. I'm sorry if I've worried you. It's just that it was such a shock to hear that name after all these years. This explains so much about all the things that have gone wrong for so long—the disappearances, the strange weather, and the conchifleurs.'

'Sir, you know who this Ogystone person is?' Suzy asked.

'Yes, I certainly do, and it isn't a person, Suzy. Oh, no. I'm ashamed to say that this Ogystone is a paxtey!'

'Wh-what!' Suzy exclaimed. So bad Paxteys do exist'

'Well, normally they don't. They make mistakes sometimes, but they would never intentionally hurt anyone or anything,' the King said with a smile.

'How did you come to know him, sir?' she asked.

'You've seen what happens when the new little ones arrive?' the King asked.

'Yes,' Suzy replied.

'Well, all paxteys arrive into the world this way, and Ogystone was no exception. There were just three paxteys that arrived in the golden basket that day, three brothers: Ogystone, Chamali, and myself.'

Suzy and Scratch both gasped in surprise.

'You see, Ogystone is the eldest, and really, if things had been different, he would have been king. The nursery nannies have told me that he was different right from the start. Everyone around him, even the animals were afraid of him. His only interest was hurting, frightening, and distressing everything around him. He caused so much destruction and unhappiness that the elders finally banished him. He never showed any remorse.' His Majesty shook his head sadly. 'Normally, a paxtey that has done something terribly wrong, especially something bad enough to cause banishment, would be so ashamed that he would puff out, and we all believed that this is what he must have done. He was banished at least a hundred and fifty years ago. I can only imagine the horrors he has inflicted over all this time.'

The King picked up his cup and stared into it, deep in thought, his face tense and sad.

After a moment, the King explained that he had sent a group of paxtey botanists to examine the conchifleurs.

'Your Majesty,' Scratch said, 'there isn't any time to waste. We must get everyone to safety before the flowers burst open, for there'll be landslides and rockfalls. I don't want to see what happened at the Capel warren happen here. Plus, they took Chamali last time, and if I'm not mistaken, the most recent threat is being organised to kidnap you, Your Majesty!' Scratch was quite panicky now, and that wasn't like him, Suzy thought, normally she was the panicky one.

'I agree with Scratch Your Majesty,' she said. 'If it is this Ogystone paxtey that's organising these terrible storms, you have to get away from here as soon as possible. You must be the target, but so many other people and creatures will be hurt, too.'

'I will go and speak with my advisors, and later, you will join us for the twilight meal,' the King said. He nodded to Scratch and Suzy and walked away.

Suzy presumed he meant that evening's dinner, and she curtseyed as His Majesty left the hall.

She and Scratch then went back outside to the courtyard, where Bira was waiting for them. He told Scratch that he and the other albatrosses had brought the little house down from the mountainside and had tucked it safely out of the way in the corner of the courtyard.

'Okay. Then, if it's all right with you, I'm going to freshen up and get ready for, erm, the twilight meal?' Suzy smiled.

'I'll come and get you when it's time.' Scratch smiled back.

Suzy went into her little house, closed the shutter over the doorway and windows, moved a cushion to the end of the bench, and lay down. She hadn't any intention of sleeping; she just needed to think.

What a day it had been, from the time that Scratch had sent the message this morning on the cliff to now, when here she was, about to have dinner with a king in his palace, on a mountain, somewhere in Northern France!

Chapter 13

The Armada of King Tobias

In no time at all, Scratch was calling for Suzy. She'd had a little wash with the water Nan had carefully stored for the purpose and changed into her best frock. She quietly thanked Nan for packing it, she never would have thought about having to dress for dinner.

As Suzy and Scratch walked along with Bira to escort them, Suzy whispered to Scratch, 'I don't understand why the King is bothering with the twilight meal when there isn't a moment to lose.'

Scratch patted her hand and calmly replied, 'You mustn't worry, Suzy. Everything is under control.'

'Oh. I see.'

Suzy didn't have time to say any more, for they then entered the hall, and what a surprise! Suzy was astonished to see how it had changed. A long table had been beautifully laid for twelve. At the far end, especially for Suzy, the King's servants had placed a human-sized table, complete with her own bouquet of flowers, and chair so that she could be comfortable. Standing on either side of the long table were five official-looking paxteys with rather serious faces. She quickly followed their lead and stood behind her chair just as King Tobias arrived.

'Good evening, sirs and Suzy. Please be seated,' His Majesty said.

The moment they had sat down, the paxtey nearest Suzy signalled to four paxteys standing at the end of the hall who would be serving the meal this evening. How smart they looked in purple suits and bow ties! They flew from guest to guest, first serving the starters of golden thyme and sage soup, and then the dinner of chestnut and broad-bean pie with marigold leaves and cranberries, followed by dessert, which was blackberry and apple jelly washed down with elderberry juice.

If Nan had tried to tempt Suzy with such an unusual menu, she would have refused, but here, she didn't like to be rude, and the food was actually quite delicious.

Perhaps Nan may be able to convert me to vegetarianism yet, she thought.

After the meal, the table was cleared.

'I do apologise for there being so few of us this evening, Suzy,' the King said with a smile.

'I'm sorry? I thought that this was your normal procedure,' Suzy replied.

'Oh my goodness, no! This hall would normally be filled to bursting for such special visitors as you,' the King said. 'However, since Scratch told us about the terrible storm and what happened to poor Chamali, it was vital that we encourage everyone to vacate the palace and their habitats. Which, I might add, is not easy!' the King said with an exasperated sigh. 'Most of our brethren feel that they can weather the storm, so we have had to send many of our supportive staff out to tell the tale of the kidnap of Chamali to convince them.'

'Thank goodness they were convinced,' Suzy replied with a sigh of relief. 'I was so worried that we were going to have to convince you to go. So where will you all go?'

'Many have already left for warrens further south and have promised to watch out for the conchifleurs,' the King replied, 'but most will cross the sea with us to safe warrens in England. I and my closest courtiers and advisors are going to the Capel Warren, where a haven is being prepared for us as we speak.'

Oh my, Suzy thought. *His Majesty is going to stay with us at Capel! I can't believe it! This is so cool.*

Everyone around the table sat quietly with their own thoughts for a moment.

'Erm, excuse me, Your Majesty,' Suzy said finally. 'May I mention something else, please?'

'Of course, please do,' the King replied.

'Not just the paxteys living in the warren were hurt by the storm; all the wildlife was affected as well. Many were killed, is there any way that we can communicate with them to warn them and maybe help them to leave, too?'

'Thank you for being so caring, but please don't fret. All the paxteys that have stayed behind to help until now are getting everything to safety.'

'So you've thought of everything, then,' Suzy said.

'I certainly hope so.' His Majesty smiled sadly. 'Now, if you will all excuse me, you all know what you have to do. Scratch will advise his friend.' The King stood up, and all the guests stood with him and bowed, except Suzy, who curtseyed.

Scratch flew over to Suzy and whispered, 'We must go and prepare for our journey back to Capel warren. I'm, so sorry that you didn't see much of the palace and grounds, but one day we will come back, and I hope we will do so at a time of celebration, and that Chamali will be with us.'

'Oh, Scratch, I hope so. I really do.' Suzy sighed.

Suzy went back to the little house and changed out of her pretty frock and into jeans and a warm top. As she sat waiting for Scratch, she looked up at the sky. Storm clouds were gathering.

Only a couple of hours left, if that, she thought. *Please, everyone hurry up and get away! I want you all to be safe, and I'm sure King Tobias will be kidnapped if he doesn't get away.*

A tap on the little house bought her back from her worried thoughts.

'Suzy, are you ready?' Scratch called. 'We will be leaving in a few moments.'

'Yes! Please hurry,' she called back.

'Before we do, I have just one more thing to ask of you.'

'And what's that?' Suzy asked.

'Will you take the babies back in the little house with you, please?'

'Wow! I didn't think there would be babies here. How many are there?'

'Six. They arrived here only a week ago, so they are very tiny. Their nurse will be staying with them.'

'I will be honoured and so proud to take them with me. Please bring them in.'

Suzy grinned from ear to ear as the babies arrived with their nurse. *Now I feel useful,* she thought. 'Please come in, ma . . . madam,' Suzy said to the nurse, trying to say it in French but hesitating in case she didn't say it properly. *I wish I had paid more attention in French classes at school,* she thought. She needn't have worried too much, however, as paxteys can understand any language.

The nurse looked concerned as she flew along in front of two other paxteys carrying the babies' basket. They set the basket down tenderly in the corner of the little house in a dip where Suzy had removed part of the seat for it to sit comfortably in.

'Thank you, Suzy. You are most kind,' the nurse said.

'You're very welcome,' Suzy said as she got the babies settled in.

'Are you ready to go?' Scratch called.

Suzy popped her head out of the doorway, as she didn't want to disturb the little ones, and responded, 'Yes, we're ready.'

Scratch looked quite worried and, Suzy thought, so did everyone else. She stepped back into the house and settled down.

'Are you comfortable, madam?' she asked the nurse.

'Yes, we are comfortable and ready. Thank you,' the nurse replied.

She and Suzy watched through the window as six paxteys dressed in the King's uniform rose into the air in a perfect line. They blew into giant shells to give the signal to go.

'Away, away, away!' called a voice in front of the little house.

'Time to go!' called more voices.

'We go, we go, and we go!' hundreds of voices answered, and the paxteys rose into the air together, the hum of hundreds of wings all around the little house.

'Away little house! follow Scratch!' Suzy shouted.

Only when she was high in the air did Suzy fully appreciate just how spectacular the King's armada truly was. They flew in a large V shape so that to any human watching from the ground with their eyes or with radar, they would appear to be a flock of geese. From Suzy's perspective, the formation was much more beautiful than that.

In the lead was King Tobias on Bira, and behind him were two albatross guards carrying the King's closest advisors and friends. Spread out behind them were the rest of the royal household, followed by every paxtey, young and old, that abided in the King's royal hamlet. Towards the back were Scratch and the little house, with Suzy and the babies and their nurse safely tucked away in little house and Scratch was close by.

Wonders of wonders! Every flying creature that had decided to leave with them, large and small, joined them, all calling to each other as they flew. Falcons, peregrines, and sparrow hawks flew with crows, jackdaws, doves and pigeons, sparrows, blackbirds, and green, red, and gold finches. They all flew together to escape the mayhem that was about to start behind them.

Suddenly, Suzy heard that awful sound that reminded her of hundreds of rusty cranes on the move, and this time, she knew what it was: the conchifleurs screeching to the clouds, encouraging them to do their worst. Then, with a mighty crash of thunder, the sky erupted with flashes of lightning. The echo of the thunder throughout the mountains made it even more fearsome.

'Oh my God, it's starting!' Suzy said, her voice trembling.

Suzy looked at the nurse, who introduced herself as Mayley, beside her. 'We are so lucky! We got away just in time,' she said, and then she looked through the peephole in the back of little house, through which she could see streaks of lightning lighting up the black sky.

As Suzy sat back down on the seat, she felt her heart pounding in her chest so hard that she could hear it. She was scared and excited all at once. The hair on the back of her neck felt like it was trying to escape, never mind stand up!, and she was covered in goose bumps. She took deep breaths and watched.

His Majesty's great armada stretched out in front of her. Little could Suzy know that back in the darkness and the thunder and lightning, a drama beyond her imagination was unfolding.

Because King Tobias was certain that there was going to be another kidnapping attempt and that he would be the victim, with the aid of his closest confidantes and guards, he had hatched a plan: twelve of his special guards remained at the palace with instruction to keep it under surveillance, and if the opportunity presented itself, they were to capture and detain the villains.

The King's special guards were magnificent paxtey specimens selected as little ones for the task. They were much taller and stronger than the average paxtey, and most importantly, they were totally loyal to the royal household and the paxtey nation. When the time was right, usually when those selected were around forty years old, they were trained to guard and protect the King in a way that would never intentionally cause others pain or make them puff out. They then volunteered for the honorary position, and those who did were revered.

These special guards had also suspected that the King would be the next kidnapping target, so they set a trap at the palace and then hid throughout the King's private quarters and the main hall and waited.

Sure enough, it wasn't long before they heard voices among the thunder, the only light from the flashes of lightning.

Kurr and Kree sneaked into the palace, sure that the noise of the raging storm outside obscured any sounds they made. These kidnapping adventures were so easy; they had become too confident for their own good.

They entered the Kings private chambers 'In here 'Kurr called to Kree. 'He must be sleeping.'

'He obviously doesn't care about his subjects if he's sleeping while they are all fighting for their lives,' Kree said.

They skulked, slowly and quietly flying across the floor.

They had come with six paxteys who had been captured from a haven in Cornwall two years previously. Even though they had lost their caring spirit, they still remembered who the King was and were scared to do such a bad thing as kidnap him, so they had decided to pretend he was an ordinary paxtey, as otherwise, it would have been hard to touch him.

There was a lump in the shape of the King bundled under the cover. He must have been fast asleep.

Kurr and Kree nodded to each other and then pounced on the bundle and pulled it out of bed only to find that it hardly weighed anything at all, so as they heaved, it lifted so easily they shot into the air. The bundle was just a sack of leaves. They and their six helpers were so shocked that they just hovered over the bed, staring at the bag.

This was exactly what the King's guards had been hoping would happen. They surrounded the intruders with a huge net.

'Now!' the captain shouted, and the net shot out and covered Kurr, Kree, and all the six other paxteys.

Ogystone's most loyal assistants had been caught!

'Aaargh, you miserable weeds; you evil snakes! Let me go! Let me out!' Kurr roared.

'How dare you! My master will slaughter you! He will get you! This will be your end!' Kree bellowed.

The guards took them and the six other poor paxteys prisoner. But those six helpers didn't care. What did it matter who their captor was, so long as they had the lovely weed to eat?

The guards gathered the prisoners together and transported them across the Channel to the Capel warren. Six blank faces stared back at them, not caring one way or the other, and Kurr and Kree continued cursing the King and his subjects to every evil known to paxteys.

When they arrived in the warren, the guards locked the prisoners in special underground rooms, with the six helper paxteys separated from Kurr and Kree in the hope that they could be helped back to normal with a special elixir that would encourage them to go into a chrysalis to hibernate. While they slept, they would be lovingly cared for by the Paxtey nurses until they emerged in three months, and it was hoped that they would have forgotten the terrible things that had happened to them and that the effects of the weed would have worn off. Kurr and Kree were to be kept imprisoned until their fate was decided by the King.

As the armada flew, Suzy watched the storm from her window and hoped that everyone had got away safely. Suddenly, the King's guards passed them at amazing speed pulling two large wooden crates.

'Scratch, what was that?' Suzy called.

Scratch joined her in the little house and told Suzy and the nurse all about the King's plan.

'I presume it went well because they were escorting prisoners.' Scratch smiled proudly.

'Oh my Do you think it's all over now?' Suzy asked.

'Not yet, they haven't found Chamali, have they?' Mayley said.

'Mayley's right,' Scratch replied. 'We will have to wait and see what happens when we get home.'

'Look! We are home!' Suzy was smiling now, as the white cliffs had come into view.

As they grew nearer, she looked for familiar sights. The warren came into sight first, and then, as she looked further up the cliff, she saw the bungalows, a big white house, and the woods. And there was Nan and Grandad's house. Suzy was so tired. The day had been so long that she felt as if she had been away for ages. She fondly glanced up and down along the cliffs, and then she caught sight of something she hadn't noticed before: a glow above the woods. It reminded her of the glow around a candle's flame. She rubbed her eyes to sharpen her vision, as she was very tired indeed. When she opened them again, she definitely saw a bright glow above the woods. The armada was heading straight for it.

It's a guiding light, that's what it is! It's welcoming us home and seeing us safely in. Thank you, whoever has lit it? I will find out tomorrow after I have slept.

Before Suzy could go home, she had to safely deposit the babies and Mayley at the new Capel nursery that had been hurriedly finished ready for the Kings arrival, so she directed the little house down into the warren and waited until someone came to meet Mayley and her little ones. Mayley thanked Suzy once more, and Suzy promised she would visit soon.

She also said goodnight to Scratch, who would be off to see His Majesty and to find out about the prisoners. Finally, she could go home.

Suzy and little house were away up in the air again over the cliff and into Grandad's garden. As Suzy landed, Nan ran up the path, lighting the way with a torch, and hugged Suzy. Together, they walked back to the house.

'Come on, love, I'll make you a nice cup of drinking chocolate. You can sit and tell us all about it,' Nan said.

Grandad greeted them in the doorway.

Suzy really was so glad to be home. She felt cosy, warm, and safe here with Nan and Grandad.

Chapter 14

Havenley Wood

Suzy was so tired after her trip that when she went to bed that night, she had told Nan that she would lie in till lunchtime. However, nature has a strange way of changing the best-made plans. As the dawn chorus started, Suzy awoke to find she was thoroughly refreshed and full of energy. She grabbed her dressing gown from the end of the bed and ran downstairs.

She didn't bother to put the kettle on, as it was much too early for tea.

'Nan and Grandad won't be up for ages yet,' she whispered to herself.

So, Suzy sat with a glass of milk and enjoyed a quiet moment reflecting on yesterday's events. She shook her head and smiled as she remembered all the amazing events and all the characters she had met. If only she could tell Julie. Suzy would have loved to share all this with her friend, and it would have been nice to have someone like herself around, for she was the odd one out in the paxtey world. Then an idea struck her: if there was anyone that could help her, it was the King.

'I know there are much more important things to think about, but this is important to me, so I'm sure he'll help me, won't he?' she whispered to herself.

As Suzy sipped her milk and dreamed, suddenly, Bang!

'Ooh!' Suzy jumped and slopped her milk over the table.

Scratch came in through the cat flap.

'Oh, Scratch, I wish you wouldn't do that! Look at the mess I've made. Can't you call out or something before bursting in?'

Scratch stood on the table and laughed as Suzy mopped up the spilt milk. She couldn't be cross with him. He was such a dear little person.

'It's so nice to see you laughing,' she said as she got the special elderberry juice that Nan kept for him in the fridge. She poured it into his tiny cup and continued, 'This is the first time I've seen you laugh since Chamali disappeared.'

'Well, there hasn't really been much to be happy about, has there?' Scratch replied.

'No, that's true.'

'But now that His Majesty is here, I feel that we have a real chance of getting Chamali back. After all, he is the King's brother and has been captured by their other brother.'

'Who would have guessed that they would be related?' Suzy said. 'Is that what you say, *related*?'

'Yes, that's acceptable. The three are brethren, bonded because they shared the same little one day.'

'I think that *related* sounds less complicated,' Suzy said with a smile. 'Scratch, I'd like to make a request to the King. How do I go about it? Am I allowed to approach him? Will you approach him for me?'

'May I ask what your request is about?'

'Well, you know how sad I am that I can't share my secret with my best friend and that it's causing such bad feelings between us. I'm wondering if he may be able to solve my problem by giving me permission to tell her about the paxteys.'

'You know,' Scratch said, 'I've been pondering over your problem, and I think there is a way for you to get your wish. I will talk with the King for you.'

'Oh, would you? It would make me so happy.'

'I think it is the least we can do for you.' Scratch smiled, walked across the table, and patted Suzy on the shoulder. 'I will go and see His Majesty right now before he gets involved with the day's affairs. Come down in the little house when you've finished first meal with Nan and Grandad. I'll see you later.'

'Okay!' Suzy called as Scratch whooshed out through the cat flap and the flap banged behind him.

'Tut-tut! If Nan and Grandad weren't awake, they will be now,' Suzy grumbled.

As soon as she could, Suzy rushed down the path to the little house, for she couldn't wait to get down to the Warren to find out how everyone had settled in and whether Scratch had been able to meet with King Tobias.

Suzy stood quietly in the doorway of the little house as it hovered just above the treetops and looked around to find His Majesty. She flew along to the small clearing and to Chamali's moss-covered storytelling rock. The sun was shining right over it.

It looks like a shrine, Suzy thought as a strong pang of sadness passed right through her middle.

As she hovered, Suzy saw all the usual paxtey groups going about their business but no sign of the King or any of his people.

'Strange. I expected to see lots of activity down here, yet it's no different from usual. I wonder where the King is. Well, I'm not going to land until I know everything's all right. I think we'll just hover here for a while, little house.' Suzy sat for a little while wondering what do.

'Oh, I'm such a fool!' she finally said. 'I'll just call Scratch quietly.'

Suzy relaxed on her bench, looked down over the treetops, and whispered as quietly as possible, 'Scratch, are you down there? Hello? Scratch, can you hear me? I'm up here in the little house, just above the treetops.' *Now we'll see if his hearing is really as sensitive as he says it is.* she thought with a smile.

Whoosh! Air rushed across Suzy's face, and then there Scratch was on the seat beside her.

'Boo!' Scratch chuckled. 'You called? Not only did I hear your whispers, but I also heard your thoughts.'

Suzy was truly impressed.

'I am going to take you to see His Majesty now. He's going to take a break from his meetings to spend some time with us. I think you will be very pleased.'

Suzy sat on the bench in little house and tried to keep calm, but it was very difficult to do, as she felt nervous again to see the King and excited about what he was going to tell her.

Scratch instructed the little house to land in the clearing by Chamali's stone. 'We will walk from here,' he said.

Suzy followed as Scratch flew up a pathway she hadn't noticed before.

It's funny that he says 'We will walk from here.' He's never walked anywhere in his life! She thought.

'I'll have you know that I do walk sometimes, but if I'm to keep at your eye level, this is the best way to travel.'

'I don't believe it! you're reading my mind again, uninvited! Will you kindly stop that?' Suzy said quite indignantly.

Scratch stopped and hovered right in front of Suzy's face.

'I do apologise, Suzy. You are right. I should not intrude into your thoughts, and I have never done so intentionally. I presume that I was meant to sense your thoughts today, but I will be much more careful in future'.

Suzy reached forward and clasped his dear little shoulders with both hands. 'It doesn't matter, really. I'm just feeling a bit touchy today. You should never have to apologise to me. We are both tired, I think. Don't you?'

'I'm sure you're right. These are difficult times.'

They carried on along the pathway, deep in their own thoughts, until they reached a clearing that was a hive of activity. Paxteys darted about in all directions, and the animals that had come with them all seemed to be busy too, digging holes and burrows. The birds darted about up in the trees, cheeping and chirping excitedly.

The part of the warren that the King and his people were staying in was hidden under a canopy of webbing, as far as Suzy could tell, although it was made from a material that Suzy was not familiar with. From the air, she could see only the trees, so it was brilliant camouflage, and whatever it was it kept them all safe from the prying eyes of enemies.

Suzy took in all the activity around her as she followed Scratch. She looked up and gasped with wonder at the shining sun and realised that she was looking through a rainbow dome.

'No wonder I couldn't see this when I flew overhead,' she whispered. 'That rainbow shield, almost a rainbow tent is protecting them. This is so absolutely amazing!'

She and Scratch stopped for a while to look around. The paxteys here had made many temporary habitats from leaves that were held together with the rainbow webbing. Each tent had a window and doorway, and inside was furniture made from fallen twigs and branches, Suzy guessed, as she knew that they would never deliberately hurt a tree. She was so full of pride for this race of little people. Even with all the awful things happening around them and to them, they still managed to house everyone and everything without damaging a single tree.

'Suzy, Scratch!' someone called.

Suzy was so engrossed in the scenery that she didn't notice the call at first, but finally she heard it when she was standing right in front of Mayley.

'Hello,' Mayley said. 'His Majesty has asked me to find you both. He is waiting for you.'

'Oh dear' Suzy said. 'I'm so sorry to have kept His Majesty waiting. We were interested to see how you had managed to house everybody, but we will be along straight away.'

Suzy walked as quickly but carefully as she could, for she didn't want to step on anyone, as she and Scratch followed Mayley along another pathway to a leafy tent bigger than the others. There was Bira standing at the doorway with the two smaller albatrosses above on a large branch of an oak tree towering over the tent, keeping watch across the warren. Bira stepped aside to allow them to enter.

'Welcome!' His Majesty said. 'Do come in.' He waved his guests to a seat.

Suzy was surprised to see the special chair that she sat on to listen to Chamali.

'I hope you have recovered from your visit with us yesterday, Suzy.'

'Yes, thank you, Your Majesty,' Suzy replied.

'Now,' the King said, 'I'm going to come straight to the point, as we have so many things to deal with, and so quickly. I have given much thought to your plight and I have asked Scratch to quietly observe your friend Julie and her family. I understand that she heard the voice in the mist not long before Chamali disappeared?'

'Yes, that's right,' Suzy replied. 'I thought that was strange because no other humans seemed to hear it but us.'

'Did your grandmother ever mention to you that Julie's mother, Sarah, was a sleep carer like your grandmother?'

'No. That's incredible! Julie's mum looked after a paxtey?'

'Yes, but tragically, he disappeared, and she believed he had puffed out. She was so heartbroken that she refused to be a sleep carer and turned from the paxteys by closing her sensitivity down so that she wouldn't be aware of our world. That was fifteen years ago. It was a very sad time. The paxtey's name was Jupee. Of course, with the knowledge we have now, we believe that he was probably kidnapped by Ogystone.' The King then lowered his voice almost to a whisper and said, 'After seeing the condition of the group of paxteys that we rescued yesterday, one can only imagine how poor Jupee must be after all this time.'

He paused for a few moments in sad reflection and then continued, 'I feel that your friend Julie is sensitive like you but hasn't had the same opportunities as you to develop her abilities. Unfortunately, since Sarah refuses to acknowledge us, we cannot contact Julie, so we have commandeered some human help. We have asked your grandmother to speak with Sarah.'

'Oh, that's so . . . so . . . I don't know what to say!' Suzy said. 'I'm so excited. Thank you, Your Majesty.'

'We shouldn't be too excited yet, for your grandmother has a difficult task ahead of her.'

'My Nan is so good at talking and listening to people that she'll bring Sarah round. I'm sure she will.' Suzy wanted to jump for joy and shout to the treetops, but she remained calm for now.

His Majesty rubbed his hands together with satisfaction. 'Yes, well . . . moving on.' He looked around as a small group of Paxtey from the French Hamlet and Capel and four of his guards gathered before him and smiled. 'Aah, here we all are, then. Now, I'm going to do something that is very pleasant for me, and I hope it will be pleasant for all of you as well. I'm going to tell you a tale that is not so much a story but a history lesson. I hasten to add that I am not as talented as Chamali when it comes to telling stories, so please be patient if I stumble a little.'

Everyone nodded and smiled and then settled down and in anticipation.

His Majesty coughed and cleared his throat then waved his hand slowly in front of himself, and a mist with a moving picture in it appeared. Suzy could see a young man walking into a barn as His Majesty began his tale.

'Many, many years ago, in the late nineteenth century to be more precise, there was a farmer called Jonas. He worked very hard on his few acres of land and dreamt of the time when he would be a rich landowner with several hundred acres.

'Late one afternoon, as he was settling the horses down after a long day working on the plough, he discovered a hibernating paxtey on one of the large beams above the hay in the barn. Of course, he didn't know it was a paxtey at the time, and he was very curious to see what kind of large insect would come out of the strange chrysalis. He decided to leave it where it was and hoped he would be there the day it hatched. He watched over it day after day and kept the straw under it clean so it would have a bed to fall on, and he kept it safe by making sure that nobody ever went near that part of the barn. He didn't want to share this amazing insect with anyone. Well, not yet, anyway.

'One Sunday morning, he was in the barn feeding his horses when he noticed the chrysalis wriggling, so he made himself comfortable in the hayloft to watch. He had misgivings about whether he had done the right thing by allowing such a large insect to stay there in the barn. What if it was something dangerous that had come across the sea from the Continent? What if it was a creature that didn't belong here? What if it was poisonous? Then, as the chrysalis split open, he noticed wings.

'"Eh, I reckon it's some kind of very large, rare butterfly," he whispered to himself.

'He rushed off and fetched a piece of blanket, because he didn't want the creature to be damaged when it dropped. He carefully arranged the blanket under the chrysalis just in time for the creature to slip out. It landed gently with a quiet plop!

'It was larger and the body of the creature was thicker than you would expect with a butterfly. He was so excited and couldn't wait to see what type of butterfly it was. But his excitement quickly turned to horror as the creature slowly rose from the blanket. There standing before him was a paxtey, the first one he had ever seen.

'At first he was so shocked that he just sat there and stared at it. The paxtey sat down and rested his little head on the straw, for it was tired after its struggle to break free from the chrysalis.

'Jonas came to his senses and realised that this was a special being that he was privileged to meet, and when he took a proper look at the paxtey's tiny, sad face, he wanted to protect him and care for him and be his friend. Whatever happened, he would make sure that none of the other farmers found out about him.

'The paxtey introduced himself as Chamali and then went on to tell Jonas all about the paxteys and their world. Just like Suzy was many years later, Jonas was invited to the paxtey haven on the first full moon of spring. Once young Jonas the farmer had discovered the world of the paxteys, he was changed forever. He learned to understand wildlife and the land around him, and he learned to work with them instead of using them and taking from them. He loved the paxtey world and his special little friend called Chamali.

'Jonas lived a long and happy life, and when he left this world in 1955, everyone was very sad, but none more than Chamali, for he had been so close to Jonas and they had shared some wonderful adventures. Before he died, Jonas had determined to leave the paxteys something that would be theirs forever, a real legacy. He owned a large area of land around Capel, so, a few years before his death, he instructed his solicitor to draw up documents to leave one of the fields nearest to the warren to the paxteys. Those documents read: "Number 10 Warrenside must be re-named Havenley. Havenley must be conserved for all time for the wildlife and must never be used by humans. Humans will only be permitted on the land if they intend to help said wildlife."

'Jonas would have preferred to say, "I bequeath Havenley to my wonderful friend Chamali", but he knew that would be impossible, so his solicitor's wording stood.

'Although Chamali continued to live in the Capel warren, he kept watch over the field called Havenley as the trees and the shrubs gradually grew wild. He watched as the badgers and the rabbits moved in along with the mice, the voles, and the moles. He watched as the foxes built their dens and the hedgehogs found safe corners to live in. A natural pond developed over an old strip of concrete, and as it got deeper and deeper, reeds appeared along its edge and frogs and newts called it home. Chamali encouraged a circle of buddleia to grow for the butterflies, and oak and ash trees grew in abundance, and so did holly bushes.

'Now here we are in 2002. Havenley has matured into a beautiful and special wood. It's special not just because it is home to many wild animals and many species of birds or because of the abundance of wildflowers. It is unique because in the centre of the woods, in a tiny sheltered grove, grow Havenley orchids. They are the only ones of their kind and have never been seen by human eyes. Until now, only two paxteys have seen them, the great Chamali and me.'

The audience responded with oohs and ahs and gasps of amazement, and King Tobias stopped talking for a while to allow everyone to digest this amazing information. Nobody could be more amazed than Suzy, however, for Havenley Woods was no more than a hundred yards from her home. She had strolled through it often with Nan and Grandad. Who would have thought that it had such an interesting history? Who would have thought that it was so special!

His Majesty raised his hands for everyone to be quiet. 'Shush, shush. I will now continue. I have almost finished the story, but there is one more wonderful part to disclose to you.

'The Havenley orchid is tended lovingly and cherished by beings not of this earth. They are spiritual beings that some would call angels. We believe that these are very old spirits of paxteys that puffed out before their time and didn't feel ready to move on, so they stay in Havenley Wood and care for everything and everyone around them. They are invisible to human eyes and to even most paxteys, for they blend in with the light of the sun. However, they do appear on very special occasions when they need us to see them and when we need help.

'I am convinced that they know about Chamali and that they would want to help, but they will not interfere unless we ask them to, so I am going into Havenley Wood this day at dusk, and, before you even ask, I will tell you that yes, I will see if we can rescue Chamali and all of Ogystone's captives.'

Everyone clapped and cheered, and many in the assembly shed tears of hope for the captives.

Suzy raised her hand. 'Sir'

'Yes, Suzy?' King Tobias said.

'Sir, if I may, I'd like to ask a question.'

'Please do.' His majesty smiled and nodded to her.

'I noticed as we approached the cliffs last night that there was a light glowing just above the woods. Would that have come from the angels in Havenley? Do you think they were welcoming us back?'

His Majesty smiled and nodded again. 'Yes. They were guiding us home. We are truly blessed to have such wonderful friends on our side.'

Suzy couldn't think of anything else to say to His Majesty that was appropriately regal, so she smiled nicely and nodded in agreement.

'I would like to thank everyone for their patience and for taking the time to listen to my tale,' the King said. 'I am sure you would all like a rest now, as do I. We will let you know when there is any further news.'

Everyone slowly left and went back to their abodes. Suzy and Scratch went back to the little house and headed home for lunch, or, as Scratch called it, noonday replenishment.

Chapter 15

The Spirit of Havenley

Suzy quickly went home to tell Nan and Grandad the story of Havenley Wood. She also had a secret yearning to see the angels, but she knew that would be very unlikely. She sighed wistfully as the little house landed in the garden. Scratch was already hovering along the garden path.

'I'm starving,' Suzy said. 'I could eat some of Nan's homemade chips in a sandwich. Mmm a chip butty!'

She went inside and found Nan and Grandad in front of the television watching the one o'clock news. The looks on their faces were enough to tell Suzy that something awful had happened.

'What's wrong?' she asked.

As Grandad turned to her and Scratch, Suzy noticed that his normally tan face was as white as a sheet. He pointed to the television. 'The weather problems have happened. Humans have put two and two together and know that the dreadful storms happen when the conchifleurs appear.'

Suzy looked at the screen as the news reader reported that not only had storms occurred all over the British Isles and Ireland but, she said, the strange plants had been spotted all across the Continent as well. Images of the devastation appeared.

'In northern France, just after these plants appeared, a storm occurred, and in the mountains, a group of climbers were injured, and one was killed,' the news reader said. 'Wildlife experts have reported that there was a mass exodus of many species of birds to southern France and to England just before the French storm struck. All wild animals in the area of the storm have disappeared completely and are presumed dead.'

The reader introduced Dr Jefferson, a botanist specialising in rare and endangered plants, and he explained that it had been impossible for researchers to study these plants, as most of them had just disappeared, and those that were picked withered and died and vanished in a puff of smoke, and although they had managed to take photographs and videos, when the photos were developed, the plants didn't appear in them, and they were also missing from the videos.

'Clearly,' Dr Jefferson said, 'we are dealing with a specimen that is unknown to us, but the world's top scientists are working to find out about them. This species has evolved before our eyes. We haven't ruled out alien life, as it isn't impossible that they may have come from a meteor of the kind that skim into our atmosphere several times a year and appear as shooting stars.'

'I'd like to pick up on that, Doctor,' the news reader said. 'Would you please explain to the viewer's how a meteor could be the source?'

'Yes, well, small rocks from outer space land on our planet frequently, and one could have carried a microscopic life form that maybe, just maybe, has bred with a terrestrial plant and produced a new rogue species. Some of our most learned and competent botanists, biologist, and other scientists are investigating the matter as we speak, and we hope to have an answer soon.'

The camera then cut from Dr Jefferson to the news reader.

'Thank you, Dr Jefferson. We will continue to monitor this story and keep you updated.'

Grandad turned the television off and turned to look at Suzy, who was standing with her mouth open, aghast! Her eyes prickled with angry tears, her stomach was in knots, and her heart thumped so fast with fear she couldn't get her breath.

'Oh no! Please don't let them find out about the paxtey world.' She looked at her grandparents with fear in her eyes for her dear little friends. 'Nan, Grandad, they won't, will they?'

Grandad spoke first. 'Scratch, you had better go and tell His Majesty at once.'

Scratch disappeared in a blink of an eye.

'Now, then,' Grandad continued, 'Let's all take a deep breath, relax, and think about this logically.'

'Okay.' Suzy nodded and plonked herself down in the armchair.

'Yes, good idea,' Nan said. 'Shall I put the kettle on?'

'Not yet,' Grandad answered. 'Let's discuss this first. 'It's the conchifleurs, not the paxteys that the humans have seen. At this moment, the paxtey world is still unknown to anyone but a special group of carers and friends, as we know. The biologists, botanists, and Uncle Tom Cobley and all, can look through their microscopes forever, but they won't ever see the paxteys, as they're not sensitive to them.'

'Of course,' Suzy agreed. 'I don't think they'll ever find the source of the conchifleurs, either. To do that, they'd have to get their hands on them to begin with, and like Dr Jefferson said they wither away and disappear in a puff of smoke.'

'Exactly,' Grandad replied. 'So, I don't think there is any reason for us to worry ourselves. Now, you can put that kettle on if you'd like.' He smiled at Nan, who showed great relief.

Whilst Nan was making tea and sandwiches, Suzy told Grandad the tale of Havenley Wood and the angels. He was so impressed that it had such a history. He said he had heard rumours about it belonging to someone and that it had to be left in its wild state, but that was all he had known.

'You know,' he said, 'I went right into the middle of those woods a couple of years ago when our gardening group volunteered to tidy up a bit, as a lot of rubbish had blown in after those gales. Do you remember?'

'Oh, yes, I do, now you mention it,' Suzy said. 'Did you notice anything unusual?'

'No. It was a peaceful wood, and I remember the pond, as we sat by it to rest. I was pleased that it was private and so overgrown that people couldn't get in there easily. There aren't many places left now that are still so totally natural. So it belongs to the paxteys, eh? Well, well, well,' Grandad said with a smile.

Scratch returned to join them for a rather late lunch, and as they all sat and munched happily, he told them the King's thoughts on the news. First, like them, he had been quite shocked by it, but after he had pondered it for a little while, he said, 'Humans only have coincidence and theory to go on, so they will never be able to connect the conchifleurs to the paxtey nation.'

His Majesty also said that he believed the paxteys were safe and that he hoped that they would find Ogystone very soon. He was sure that the conchifleurs would disappear once they could solve this problem.

'One more thing,' Scratch said. 'As you know, Suzy, the King is going into Havenley Wood later, and he has invited me to go with him and has asked if you would care to join us.'

'Yes! Of course! What a question. Who would say no?' Suzy answered.

'His Majesty said he didn't know if the angels would appear in front of you and allow you to see them, so he couldn't promise that you will see anything at all. However, he knows and they will know that your intentions are purely good. We will see.'

'Wow! Yes!' Suzy clapped. She was thrilled. What an honour to be invited by the King!

'We are going in at dusk. I will come and fetch you when it is time,' Scratch said.

'I'll be ready,' Suzy replied.

It was mid-afternoon by the time they had finished lunch and Scratch had gone back to the warren, and Suzy thought she would go up to her room for some quiet time when Nan stopped her.

'With all this excitement, I forgot to tell you that Julie is coming round to see you this afternoon at four o'clock.'

'She is? Did she phone?'

'Well, I went round to visit her mum. Sarah and I had a long chat about what happened all those years ago. It was a good sign, I thought, because she wouldn't even talk about it before. I reminded her about her friend Jupee and said that it was possible he may not have puffed out after all.'

'Blimey Nan! What did she think about that?'

'She was shocked, but she is still determined not to be involved with the paxteys anymore. I have to respect her decision, don't I?'

'Yes, of course you do,' Suzy answered.

'I then asked her if she knew that Julie was showing signs of being sensitive, and Sarah said that she had a feeling Julie was aware of the paxteys but hadn't encouraged her sensitivity because she didn't want Julie to go through the heartbreak that she had experienced when her relationship with Jupee came to an end.'

Nan paused and then continued, 'Anyway, we talked for a long time. I told her about all the things that had happened to the paxteys lately and how much they need our help. I think it made her realise that maybe she should reconsider her decision. I left her to think about things, and just before I left Julie told me she was excited to see you, so I told her to come round at four o'clock'

'Yes! At last! Oh, thanks, Nan.' Suzy Gave Nan a big hug. 'I can't believe it that my mate and I will be able to do things together again.'

'Now hold on a minute, Suzy, and come back down to earth,' Nan said, putting both hands up in the air. 'Julie may know about the paxteys, but she needs time to meet them and to learn about them. You can't just plunge her in at the deep end. The paxteys will have to get to know her, too, and she also needs a paxtey friend of her own. In other words, she will have to wait till someone chooses her. You know that, don't you?'

'How stupid of me,' Suzy replied. 'You're absolutely right. And with all this serious stuff going on, I don't imagine there will be much time for welcoming parties,' Suzy replied. 'But for now I'll be able to tell her everything that has happened to me and introduce her to Scratch, won't I?

'Yes, I'm sure that will be okay and that Scratch will help you,' Nan said.

Julie arrived at four o'clock on the dot. Suzy rushed to the door, and as she opened it, Julie ran in and nearly knocked her over.

'I can't believe it! Suzy, this is incredible! My mum has told me all about you and your grandparents being involved with these little people and that once, a long time ago, she was involved too!'

'Yes, now calm down. I know it's a shock and a lot to take in. Come on. We'll go into the dining room and I'll tell you all about it.'

Suzy and Julie sat there just the two of them for the next hour sipping Diet Pepsis, talking, giggling, and occasionally shouting, 'No! I don't believe it. Get out!'

Once Suzy got to the serious part about the captured paxteys and the plan to rescue them, Julie was quiet and listened carefully. When Suzy had finished, she said that she knew with absolute certainty that she was meant to be a part of this world just as Suzy was; she could feel it deep in her soul. As Suzy talked about the paxteys, she saw these dear darling people in her head, and she had seen them often in her dreams, so she wouldn't be shocked when she met them.

'Now, I haven't got a lot of time left, as I've got to have dinner and get ready for tonight,' Suzy said, 'but I want to do one thing first. Come with me to the garden.' She jumped up and grabbed Julie's hand.

Julie followed without a word down the garden and to the little house.

'Julie, this is the little house. Come in and make yourself comfortable.'

Julie sat down and looked around. 'This is really nice and comfy, isn't it?' She sat and tapped the seat beside her.

'It has to be. You see . . . it flies.' Suzy smiled.

'It *what?*'

'I'll show you tomorrow. Next, I'm going to introduce you to Scratch.'

'Is he here?' Julie asked excitedly as she looked around.

'Not yet, but he'll be here very shortly.' Suzy stepped outside and turned towards the warren.

'Scratch, are you there?' Suzy whispered. 'I need to see you. If you have time, could you come to the little house in the garden, please?'

'You're speaking so quietly,' Julie said. 'Will he be able to hear you?'

'Yes, he only has to—'

Whoosh! Scratch appeared.

Julie jumped. 'Oh!'

Suzy smiled with pride and introduced her friend

Scratch smiled and bowed in mid-air. 'I am most honoured to meet you, Julie.'

'I am delighted to meet you,' Julie whispered.

To say that she was overwhelmed would have been an understatement. She just had to sit and stare to take in this incredible creature in front of her. Suzy remembered how she felt the first time she saw Scratch and knew that she had to give Julie a little time even though she was staring. She looked utterly mesmerised.

'Are you all right?' Suzy said, waving her hand in front of Julie's face.

Julie shook her head to wake herself up and said, 'I'm sorry, Scratch. I didn't mean to be so rude by staring, but I have never seen a paxtey.'

'It's quite all right, Julie. I understand,' Scratch said. 'Do you have any questions for me? I can stay for a little while.'

'Erm . . . There's so much to think about . . . so much to take in!' Julie exclaimed.

'It's all right, Ju. That's just how I was when I first met Scratch. I know just how you feel.' Suzy linked arms with her friend. 'How about we call it a day so you have time to think about everything? Maybe we can meet up later.'

Julie nodded and smiled at Scratch and then Suzy. 'I'll go home and chat to Mum. Thank you for seeing me, Scratch. I can't imagine what you must think of my silly behaviour!'

Scratch hovered and smiled at the two friends interesting display of camaraderie. He had understood their friendship and Suzy's need to have her friend around. Now as he looked at the two of them together he knew the decision to find a way for Julie to be involved was right. His paxtey senses showed him that their spirits would be linked forever.

'Do not concern yourself, Julie. I look forward to a time when we can relax and get to know each other properly. Now I must go. Suzy, I will see you at dusk,' he called, and then there was a puff of wind on Suzy's and Julie's faces and he was gone.

With a wonderful feeling of relief, Suzy watched her friend disappear up the lane waving as she went. At last she didn't have to keep secrets.

She then ran indoors and upstairs. She didn't have long before dusk, and she wanted to bathe and freshen up so she would be respectable when she met the angels of Havenley that night.

In no time at all, Suzy had finished, Scratch was back, and they were walking down the lane towards Havenley Wood. Suzy's stomach fluttered anxiously and she noticed that Scratch had his I'm-busy-thinking look on his face as he flew beside her silently. She sensed that he was as nervous as she. By the time they reached the footpath into the woods, dusk was ending and night was closing in quickly. King Tobias reached the footpath just as they did.

'Good evening, Suzy,' His Majesty said.

'Good evening, sir,' Suzy replied with a quick nervous curtsey.

His Majesty hovered in front of Suzy and Scratch and said, 'As you can probably imagine, I have given some considerable thought to how we will manage this visit to the Havenley angels. I'm not sure yet whether they will receive me as a visitor, so we must proceed with caution. I will go on ahead with Scratch, and Suzy, you will shadow us and watch for our signals. Will you be all right with that?'

'Yes, I will be fine. I'll stay in the background.'

The King then moved into the woods, followed by Scratch almost level with him on his right. Suzy followed a few feet behind. Any daylight that was left slowly disappeared as they walked deeper into the woods.

Suzy wondered how they were going to follow the path in the darkness, but just as the thought popped into her head, a glow appeared under her feet and along the pathway ahead. She stopped for a second just to look.

'They are showing us the way!' she whispered quietly to herself.

Suzy, please, not even a whisper, His Majesty said in her head. She nodded and apologised silently.

She stood and gazed at the pale yellow luminous pathway. The light had to be marking the way, so she looked down at her feet and then followed the light very slowly. When she looked ahead to where the pathway seemed to end, she noticed a light lift into the air, and as it did, so the colour changed to a pulsating opalescence. It moved towards them, and then, behind it, another and, yes! Another followed.

Very soon dozens of orbs pulsated all around them, were leading the way and keeping them company. Suzy then heard the gentle sound of wind chimes and angelic voices. She didn't feel scared or even nervous anymore; instead, a warm sense of well-being spread through her. She knew she would be welcomed here. She could see where she was walking very clearly now, as the light from these orbs made the path as bright as day.

Well ahead of Suzy, His Majesty and Scratch were guided into a clearing, at the entrance of which was a pathway of living light, beating like a heartbeat, leading to the Havenley orchid in perfectly kept beds, it's exquisite pink, blue, and purple blooms bathed in light. His Majesty and Scratch hovered a few inches above the pathway to admire the beauty before them.

Suzy followed an orb towards the edge of the clearing, and when it stopped just in front of her, she understood that this was as far as she could go. She sat on a log and gazed in disbelief at the sight in the clearing, at the pulsating path of light and that magnificent wall of multi-coloured orchids they were beyond anyone's imagination. Then, wonder of wonders! Suzy had to put her hand over her mouth to stop any noise from escaping.

It was a real angel; it just had to be, although this angel wasn't like any of the pictures she had seen at school. Instead of a human being with wings, this angel had many rays of light in constant motion which could have been mistaken for wings. It was hard to say where the being within the rays began and ended. Suzy saw loving eyes and a comforting smile and felt overwhelming peace.

His Majesty and the angel were engaged in a silent conversation, and Suzy heard every word in her head.

'Welcome Tobias. 'King Tobias bowed deeply

'We have followed your progress since you last visited Havenley with your brother Chamali and have seen that you have carried out your responsibilities as King of the paxtey nation with great dignity and wisdom.'

'Thank you, His Majesty replied. Your observations would fill me with pride were it not for the sadness we are experiencing now.'

'We are aware of the darkness that has befallen the world, the angel said, and you are here to request our help, are you not?'

'Yes, we are.' His Majesty bowed his head sadly but then took a deep breath and continued, 'Are you aware that many paxteys, including my brother Chamali, have disappeared? And are you also aware that my other brother Ogystone seems to be responsible?'

'Indeed, we are very well aware. We would not usually interfere, as we are here only to support and counsel; however, no human or paxtey will be able to correct this situation without help from our side.'

There were a few seconds of silence as the angel considered her next words carefully. 'You see, Tobias,' she said, 'you have just one brother, Chamali. Ogystone is not a paxtey or a human. This creature is not of this world. He is the essence of evil that appeared in the basket with you and Chamali under the rainbow and has lived here in physical form for nearly two hundred years. His sole purpose has been to destroy all happiness, all goodness and make everything that is beautiful ugly. He thrives on misery and pain. Unfortunately for you, he spent the first fifty years of his life living in the happy world of the paxteys, which revolted him and made him even more determined to destroy, and now his plan to destroy life on this planet also includes blaming his destruction on the paxtey nation, particularly you as the King.'

Suzy watched in horror as His Majesty sank to the ground with his head in his hands.

'All those people and paxteys going missing, those animals lost and killed—that all happened because of his hatred for me? The terrible storms carried out in the name of revenge?' His Majesty's voice trembled.

Tears welled up in Suzy's eyes. The King was so good and kind; he didn't deserve to have this awful burden heaped upon him.

The King cried out in anguish.

'No, no, Tobias!' the angel's voice called out above. 'This is not for revenge. Ogystone would have done all these terrible things whether you existed or not. He will try to ruin you by heaping blame on you, so you cannot and must not hold yourself responsible.'

More silence as His Majesty digested all this information. Scratch turned to look at Suzy, and he looked as shocked as the King. Suzy returned a look of sympathy and love with her tearful eyes. Then the King lifted his head and slowly stood up and then hovered above the ground. His expression had changed: although it was still grim, it now showed determination.

'It would seem that we the paxteys must right the wrongs that have been done to this world of ours, and quickly, before any more lives are lost!' the King said.

'Yes, Tobias. I'm glad we agree. You will have our help.'

'Thank you,' His Majesty replied.

The angel then said, 'you must gather your strongest guards, your bravest paxteys, and as many humans as you can. It is time to rid the world of this evil being. You will have to be angry and forceful and may even need to hurt the being—you will have to fight. First, go and build your army, and then come back to me. I will give you the special weapon that you will need to complete the task.'

The rays of light faded behind the angel, and she disappeared as orbs gathered around the King, Scratch, and Suzy showing them the way out of the Havenley Wood. Suzy took one last look at the orchids and followed His Majesty and Scratch. The orbs bobbed along with them lighting the way until they reached the edge of the woods. When Suzy stepped onto the road, she looked behind her just in time to see the light from the orbs go out as if someone had switched them off. She stood with Scratch and King Tobias for a while as their eyes adjusted to the dark, and then Suzy remembered that she was carrying a pocket torch and hurriedly switched it on.

'We must call an extraordinary meeting,' the King said to Scratch.

'Yes, Your Majesty,' Scratch replied.

'I would like you to go as quickly as possible to the two nearest warrens to invite their leaders to a meeting at dusk tomorrow; ask them to pass the word on across the land and across the sea to the Irish warrens.'

Scratch agreed and called to Suzy, 'We'll speak later!' And with a whoosh! He was gone before Suzy could even answer.

'Suzy, you must go straight home and tell your grandparents everything that you have heard,' King Tobias said. 'They will know what they have to do. I will see you shortly, and I thank you for your company.'

'It was my pleasure,' Suzy replied with a quick curtsy.

Whoosh! His Majesty was gone, and Suzy was alone with her torch.

'The King has left the building,' Suzy said to herself with a giggle as she turned and started to jog home. 'That was so cool. I have never seen anything so amazing in my life, and I probably won't again. How many people get to see a real angel, I wonder?'

She was so excited as she turned the corner into her lane and approached her house that she jumped over the fence into the garden, her arms up, shouting, 'Wa*hoo!*'

CHAPTER 16

The King's Army

As Suzy burst through the kitchen door, breathless and excited at the thrill of seeing an angel, she expected to find Nan and Grandad waiting for her and was pleasantly surprised to find that Julie and her mum, Sarah, were there as well.

Breathless, Suzy sat at the table and sipped hot chocolate made with cream and told everyone everything she had heard and seen, her audience oohing and ahing, and she finished with the instructions from the King for Nan and Grandad.

'What did he mean when he said you would know what to do?' Suzy asked.

'It's time to contact the Twelve,' Grandad said to Nan. 'I think we'll do that straight away.' He went into the living room with Suzy close on his heels.

'What Twelve? Who are they?' Suzy asked.

Suzy was puzzled as Grandad went to the big dresser in the dining room, reached deep into the back of the cupboard, pressed a button, and slid open a secret panel to reveal a safe. He took out a map and a small mother-of-pearl box, lifted the lid, and pressed another button inside.

Suzy then heard *whoo-ee, whoo-ee, whoo-ee,* which wasn't unpleasant, yet she could tell it signalled something urgent, and that she was being called. The sound continued in her head in bursts of three, with a three-second pause between bursts. Then, after three minutes, it stopped altogether.

'What on earth is that noise in my head?' Julie asked as she came into the room.

Sarah and Nan said that they had heard it as well but didn't seem surprised.

'Just you wait and see, love,' Nan told Julie. 'It's the signal. Watch how quickly everyone responds.'

'Everyone? Suzy said. 'You mean more people like us?'

Nan smiled and nodded just as the phone rang. She handed a cup of tea to Grandad, who answered the phone, and then sat down with her own mug.

'You see, at least two humans like us are connected to every warren across the British Isles, and these humans decided many years ago to nominate one person to initiate contact among them all. Grandad has a map of all the warrens and you'll see it is divided into twelve regions, and one human from each of these regions is responsible for communication, and that signal is how we communicate with the other eleven in an emergency.'

Suzy was completely taken back, as it hadn't occurred to her that other human beings living near other warrens would be involved in the paxtey world.

'I'm so amazed,' Suzy said. 'I thought that we were the only ones who knew about the paxteys.'

'Well, consider that if there are four of us attached to the Capel warren, there must be several hundred humans working for the paxteys across the British Isles if there are at least two people like us for each warren, and they all keep the secret.' Nan smiled proudly.

Suzy then listened to Grandad's side of the phone conversation.

'Sean? Hello, mate. It's just as we thought . . . Yes . . . Hmm . . . Yep, that's right, it's time for the gathering. So we'll see you here tomorrow? Okay. Bye.' Grandad rang off and ticked off the first name on the list written on the map of the British Isles he had spread out on the kitchen table.

'That was Ireland! We're away now,' he said to everyone in the kitchen. The phone rang again.

'Hello? Yes, Dougal, thanks for being so prompt . . . Yes; just what we've been waiting for . . . Capel warren tomorrow at dusk . . . Okay, I'll see you then. Bye.'

As he replaced the receiver, the phone rang again. Everyone assembled listened, fascinated.

'Hello, Dyfed . . . Yes, everyone's meeting at the Capel warren at dusk tomorrow. Yes, that's right it is . . . His Majesty will be there . . . Mmm . . . We will all gather here first, right look forward to seeing you, then. Bye.'

He rang off and called out, 'That was Wales!'

After two hours, Grandad had finally spoken to all twelve people on his list from Northern and Southern Ireland, Scotland, Wales, the West Country, the Isle of Wight, the New Forest and Southampton area, Suffolk, Norfolk, the Shetland Isles, and the Isle of Man. Grandad was the representative for the southeast.

'Right they are all on their way' he said to Nan.

'Well, then,' Nan said as she turned to Suzy. 'It's all hands on deck. We have much to do.'

The next twenty-four hours passed so quickly. That evening, Suzy's family and friends didn't get to sleep until the early hours of the morning, as the phone continued to ring as people had more questions and news. Everyone had an opinion on what would happen next, on how King Tobias and his army would deal with Ogystone, some of them were even suggesting that they had inside knowledge. Finally, Grandad slammed the phone down wearily.

'You always get one, don't you? There's always one know-all who thinks he knows more than anyone else!'

Poor ol' Grandad. He's so tired, Suzy thought as she dozed off in the armchair where she sat to keep him company.

'Now, now, love,' Nan said with a smile, 'let's get off to bed. Everyone can wait till the morning.'

The next day carried on in the same chaotic way as Grandad prepared to meet the eleven other representatives and answered the continuously ringing phone, and Nan, Suzy, Julie, and Sarah rushed around to get the house ready. Everything had to be squeaky clean, and they had to prepare food and enough chairs with comfortable cushions. Nan opened the partition between the living room and dining room to create a large reception room for everyone.

By three o'clock the house was finally ready and the first visitor arrived, from Scotland, Each human had travelled to Capel with the paxtey leaders from every warren in his area. The paxteys went straight down to the Capel warren, where they were expected.

Whilst Nan and Suzy busied themselves serving refreshments, the representatives discussed what the King would do and should do.

'If I were him . . .' said one of them, Suzy presumed it was the know-all Grandad had talked about last night.

At long last, dusk arrived, and the Twelve set off for the meeting in pairs at three-minute intervals so they wouldn't attract attention. Julie, Suzy, and Grandad were last to leave, and Nan and Sarah stayed behind to prepare for everyone's return.

Suzy was so excited that she had difficulty remaining calm and in control. As she reached the last step down to the warren, the sight before her was spectacular.

The rainbow shield around the warren had been strengthened so that the large assembly of people, paxteys, and animals couldn't be detected from the ground or the air.

King Tobias stood on a branch of the old oak tree, where he was much higher than anyone else so everyone could see him and hear him. Bira, his constant guard, stood on a branch above him and six of the King's special guard stood on either side of him, and his scribes sat on lower branches, ready to make notes as he spoke. Grandad also had his notepad at the ready.

Suzy sat on a tree branch with Julie, and for once they were both speechless because there was so much to marvel at. Sadness overwhelmed Suzy as she looked at the old oak tree, Chamali's home.

'I hope he's okay. Please don't let him be hurt and suffering or changed like those rescued paxteys we saw,' she whispered to the trees.

As Suzy's thoughts went out across the airwaves, Chamali was safe. He was far from happy or comfortable shut away in his horrible stony cell, but he was unharmed.

True to his word, Ogystone had left him locked away in hope that he would finally give up and puff out in despair, and to speed up the process, Ogystone hadn't left him in peace. As often as he had been able, Ogystone had come to taunt Chamali and call him appalling names, and he had sent his slaves along to whisper hateful messages.

'They say that Chamali is cowardly, that he flew away when the storm came, and that he was too scared to stay through hard times,' one slave said.

'Your friends hate you now,' another said. 'They don't want you back.'

Chamali, still safe in his rainbow shield, didn't believe a word. He knew his friends would never think such things. However, he got very worried when Ogystone taunted him about the big storm in the mountains of France, saying the conchifleurs had been planted and were ready to blow.

Chamali sent the thought, *please help everyone there and keep them safe*, over the airwaves.

A few days later, he heard Ogystone's roaring voice echo through the passageways, and he was sure Ogystone was on his way to get him.

He prepared himself as Ogystone bellowed, 'I'm going to kill them all! I will send such a mighty storm that it will wipe out half the world! Many will drown, and those that don't will be happy to puff out to get away from the destruction! Tobias will rue the day they took my men away!'

The rant continued for most of the night and the next day, when Peeps the bat arrived with food, just as he had every day Chamali had been imprisoned. He brought berries and edible flowers and an unusual-tasting liquid to drink, carried in a tiny ball. Chamali didn't know what it was, but Peeps assured him that it was good for him, so he drank it.

Poor Chamali had become so disorientated that he hadn't noticed until now that Peeps had got bigger and that the hole in the ceiling had got farther away and much wider than it had been.

'Thank goodness you are still coming to see me, my dear little Peeps,' Chamali said when he heard the bat fly in. When Chamali turned round, he was stunned to see that Peeps was now bigger than he was.

'Peeps! You've grown so huge!'

'No, my friend, I am still the same size. It is you that has shrunk. That liquid I've given you to drink came from the Havenley angels, and it will allow me to get you out of here and to take you home before Ogystone comes for you. King Tobias has planned an invasion, and when Ogystone realises what is happening, he will not let you live.'

Chamali let out a big sigh of relief and fought back the tears welling up in his eyes. 'Thank goodness!'

'Come, now. I'll help you.'

As Chamali stood up and moved towards Peeps, he was very wobbly, as he hadn't moved for a very long time. Peeps then carried him to the hole in the ceiling.

'You will be able to fly once we are through this tunnel,' Peeps said. 'Just hold on to me for now.'

Chamali held on as Peeps flew. It seemed as if the black tunnel would never come to an end, but at long last, he saw daylight, and cold, thick, foggy air took his breath away. He was free! With great effort, whoosh!

he was off and flying. Peeps led Chamali back to Havenley, as instructed, where the angels would care for him until he had regained his strength.

Suzy took a deep breath and tried to shake off the sadness for Chamali and concentrate on the scene around her. She adjusted her focus on the trees and saw that they were now full of paxteys along with many different species of birds, from tiny sparrows and finches to huge owls and kestrels, all of them straining to get a good view of the King. On the ground in a circle nearest the tree sat paxteys with the young ones, and behind them stood the nurses with the youngest babies. Finally, the humans stood on the outside. The audience was so large that Suzy wouldn't have been able to count everyone, but she knew their numbers had to be in the hundreds and hundreds.

The King raised his hands, and the audience quieted and listened.

'My dear friends,' the King said, 'Thank you all so much for coming today. It cheers me to see so many of you and makes me believe that we have the strength and resources to win this battle. I trust you all understand everything that has happened so far.' He paused as everyone nodded or said yes.

'Then you know just how bad the storms were and how many people have disappeared. There's not a warren anywhere that hasn't been hit by one of these tragedies. Therefore, it is time to gather our forces and fight back.'

He paused again, and many responded with shouts of agreement and nods.

King Tobias raised his hands again. 'It is hard for me and all paxteys to think about fighting, as we are not an aggressive race.

Duncan McFarlane, the Scottish human representative, called out, 'Dinne fret, Your Majesty. We'll be aggressive fur ye!'

'In our own ways, we must all be equally strong.' The King waved his arm in the air, and a huge image appeared above the audience showing a mountain covered in mist The King and his army of paxteys and humans had gathered in a horseshoe shape, with the King, Bira, and the King's guard at the curve of the horseshoe, at the head of the army, the paxteys were inside the horseshoe, and the humans, with the most physical might, following at the rear on the outside of the horseshoe. The birds, including kestrels, buzzards, eagles, owls, and seagulls, were to be the eyes and ears of the army, as well as a distraction for the enemy, as they flew above the mountain.

Those assembled in the warren expressed much excitement as they viewed the plans for such a large army, but King Tobias remained serious and explained that they would experience some difficulties that they may not understand. 'The sad fact that we must all face is that there are some of our captured friends who will not want to be rescued.'

Murmurs of, 'Huh?' and 'What does he mean?' passed through the audience.

'Some of our friends have been gone for many seasons during which they have been fed and given drink by a devious enemy. A mineral in the water that runs into the inner caverns of the mountain changes the way that vegetation inside the caverns grow. These plants look like the lovely food that we eat in our warrens, but those in the mountain are toxic to paxteys and take away their spirits and their loving natures, leaving them no longer caring about anything or anyone. They become dependent on what they call "the humble weed", so they will do anything to serve their master to get it. Therefore, many of them won't want to be rescued because they will no longer be able to have the humble weed, and we are going to have to force them to come home with us.' He paused. 'And yes, we could find ourselves fighting our own people.'

Everyone was quiet and many looked shocked.

His Majesty continued, 'We will have some extra help from the Havenley angels, but we won't know what that is going to be until we set off. I'm also given to understand that there are some paxteys locked away in caverns away from the main mountain that will also need to be rescued. So, we will need to decide who will go in breakaway groups and to plan for these other paxteys' rescue. But for now, I think we will take a little break for refreshment and discussion. In a while, I will pass among you and discuss your individual needs.'

After a moment of silence, everyone started to talk at once. It hadn't occurred to any of the paxteys that the friends they had lost might not want to come home, and they were so confused that His Majesty spent a long time amongst them in an attempt to explain the situation to individuals.

Grandad did understand this unfortunate concept, and so did the other humans, so they stood aside and watched the discussions, some of them saying they felt a twinge of sadness.

Eventually, His Majesty made his way to Grandad and the rest of the Twelve.

'Here we are, then,' the King said, hovering at the humans' eye level so he could be seen. 'I'm so sorry I've taken so long.'

'That's quite all right,' Grandad replied.

'Do you have any questions for me?'

'Yes,' Grandad said. 'With such a huge army crossing the sky, how will we escape detection by human radar?'

'The Havenley angels will protect us with a shield which will hide us not only from the humans but also from Ogystone's cohorts on the mountain.'

Suzy then raised her hand, and the King turned his attention to her.

'If you please, Your Majesty, what will happen to the paxteys that we bring home with us, especially those that do not want be rescued?'

'Well,' the King said, 'we have many nurses that don't have any new babies to care for, so when the kidnapped paxteys come home, we will put all of them into hibernation, and the nurses will watch over them and care for them until they awaken in three months. Whilst they sleep, we will also identify them. Unfortunately, none of us can possibly know what state they will be in when they wake.'

'You certainly seem to be well informed about Ogystone Mountain,' Grandad said. 'I presume you got this information from paxteys who were recently rescued.'

'Yes, that was the source of some of our intelligence, but most of what we know comes from Peeps, Chamali's pet bat, who has been visiting Chamali.'

'Oh, please tell us about Chamali!' Suzy said. 'Is he well? Will he have been given the humble weed like those other paxteys?'

'Well, now, I'm not able to tell you much. I only know that as we speak, his friend Peeps is helping him to escape. I'm given to understand that he hasn't changed as the others have, but we will have to be patient and see how he is when he comes home, which I know will be soon.'

Everyone cheered and clapped in delight, and Scratch appeared at Suzy's side, smiling and laughing joyfully.

The good news about Chamali seemed to lift everyone's spirits, and they were now more positive than ever. Suddenly going to Ogystone Mountain to rescue their friends from that terrible Ogystone didn't seem impossible.

In forty-eight hours, at 3 a.m. on Saturday, the army would head north, and the early start meant that they would be on their way with most of their journey completed before sunrise. Five hundred paxteys would travel with the King, Bira, and, of course, the King's elite guards. Thirty-six humans, including the Twelve, would also accompany them.

King Tobias expressed a quiet hope that the army would be large enough and that their courage and determination would serve as weapons, because they didn't seem to have anything else with which to fight. He also explained that he would visit Havenley tonight to receive protection for his people and the humans. The angels had also promised him a weapon, but he didn't want to kill.

Finally, after answering many more questions, the King went back to the branch of the big oak tree so that everyone could see him, and silence prevailed once more.

'I am sure the Havenley angels would not allow us to embark on such a venture unless we were properly equipped, so I ask all of you to trust that they will keep you safe. I will see you on Saturday morning, when, at last, we will set off together to rescue our friends!'

Everyone human and paxtey cheered, and when they had settled down, they made their way home. All members of the Twelve plus Suzy and Julie went back to Nan and Grandad's for tea, fruit juices, and homemade cakes and sandwiches. As they ate and drank, there was further discussion and much misgiving about what sort of weapon the angels would give them, and they expressed concern about fighting, but if it came to it, they all agreed they would.

Finally, everyone left, and Nan, Grandad, and Suzy, finally alone, crashed into armchairs, absolutely exhausted.

'King Tobias's incredible army really is going to be something to see,' Suzy said. 'I'm trying to imagine how the plan will work, but I just can't visualise it. Can you?'

Nan answered in a tired whisper,' 'Yes, I can see it very clearly. I know it will work and that you'll all come back safe and sound. I can feel it.'

Chapter 17

The Invasion of Ogystone Mountain

The next forty-eight hours flew by for Suzy, as there was so much to organise and pack into the little house. Nan kept thinking of one more thing, 'Just in case,' she said.

Finally it was Saturday morning, and at precisely ten minutes to three, everyone had assembled in and around the warren. They had all studied the formations and knew their positions. They were ready.

The paxteys hovered silently a few feet off the ground, and the King hovered slightly higher and faced them. Behind the paxteys, the humans waited in their various flying machines. The only sound was the rustling of leaves in the breeze; even the birds were quiet.

Suzy then recognised the sound of the angels' chime that she had heard in Havenley Wood. Sure enough, the orbs dashed into the warren, that wonderfully bright opalescent light flitting round and round as they circled the people, paxteys, and animals faster and faster.

All stayed silent and still as they watched the orbs. It was a brief but peaceful moment. The troops' fears disappeared and were replaced by positivity. Everything was going to be all right now. Then, as suddenly as the orbs had appeared, they were gone.

Twelve of the King's trumpeters then rose into the air and sounded the rallying call.

'It is time to rescue our friends!' the King cried. 'Away! Away!'

Everyone cheered and cried in response, away, away we go!'

'Wagons roll!' Grandad called out, and the little house rose.

The King, on Bira, set off first, flanked by his two albatross bodyguards and his twelve elite guards. Then an incredible sound that could have been mistaken for a jet engine filled the air as five hundred sets of wings flapped and the paxteys took off all at once. The humans took off next, and the birds followed at the rear.

It wasn't until they were high up in the air and flying at a steady pace that Suzy could finally relax a little and take in the scene in front of her.

'Phew! I've just realised that I've been holding my breath since we set off. Oh my!' she squealed. 'Will you look at that?'

The forces had assembled into the horseshoe shape, just like in the King's plans, and a long way ahead Suzy spotted His Majesty on Bira flanked by the other albatrosses. The elite guards had shifted into a semicircle around the King, and behind them flew the paxteys in ten neat rows of fifty, and this was where the neatness ended.

Suzy laughed. 'Look at the humans' ranks!'

Most of the humans had chosen motorbikes as their flying machines, and Grandad identified them as everything from a very smart sporty Suzuki to a very old AJS 250. Then there was a telephone box, a small garden shed, eight microlights, and even a little car that opened up at the front called a bubble car. Grandad reminded Suzy that they were there for an important task, no matter how funny they looked.

In the little house, Suzy and Grandad were quite cosy, and Suzy hoped everyone else was feeling as comfortable as she was because they had a heck of a long way to go—at least six hours, Suzy estimated—even though they were flying really fast.

Grandad had invited Sarah to come along as his other helper because she might be able to rescue her paxtey friend Jupee. After being away from the paxtey world for so long, she was so sorry she had been so selfish, and she explained that if she had known Jupee had been kidnapped, she would have tried to find him much sooner.

Suzy was also glad that Sarah had come, and she knew that together, the three of them would make a great team.

Suzy settled back with a breakfast sandwich that Nan had packed and thought about Scratch. She wished he could ride in the little house with her. No sooner had she thought that and taken her next bite than he was by her side.

'Did Nan pack anything for me, by any chance?' he asked.

'I didn't think I would see you during the journey!' Suzy said. She picked a little plastic box out of the bag marked 'Scratch' that Nan had packed and handed it to him. 'Nan did pack something for you. You don't think she would forget you, do you?'

Scratch found a breakfast of berries and nuts and elderberry juice, and as he munched, he explained that His Majesty had instructed him to leave the line to tell those in the little house the next part of the plan.

When they arrived at Ogystone Mountain, he said, they would find three entrances. Suzy, Grandad, and Sarah nodded, as they had seen this on the map.

'His Majesty asked me to remind all of you that in addition to the shield around our whole group, you each have your own individual shield and you cannot be physically hurt as long as you remember it is there.'

He then waved to the bench the humans were sitting on. 'Under the seat you will find a box containing three giant nets. Twelve humans with such a net will go into each tunnel accompanied by one hundred and fifty paxteys. His Majesty will go ahead with his guards and fifty paxteys to deal with Ogystone. He asked me to say that whatever you see, no matter how strange it is, please ignore it and concentrate on gathering up our kidnapped paxtey friends with the net.' Scratch closed his food box and handed it back to Suzy. 'I must go now. I won't see you again until we get to the mountain.' He hovered in the doorway of the little house and looked at Suzy. 'If you follow all our instructions and remember your shield, you will be safe. Please don't stray from the plan.'

Suzy nodded and then smiled and waved as he took off.

She and her companions sat quietly for a while, mulling over the things that Scratch had told them.

'Scratch was talking about nets and gathering as if we were fishing,' Suzy said.

'I think that catching the kidnapped paxteys in the net will be a bit like that,' Sarah replied.

Suzy was worried. 'Doesn't that seem a bit cruel?'

'Of course not, let's have a look at the nets to see what they're like,' Grandad said. He lifted up the side of the seat where the storage bin was and mentioned that he didn't remember seeing anything in there besides their own things last night and that he wondered when the nets could have been added.

'Well, I'll be. Just look at this!' He marvelled at the bin.

Suzy and Sharon peered in, and Suzy saw a pile of netting unlike any fishing net, for this was made from a delicate material that looked like spider webs in the early morning dew, sparkling with gold and white light. Grandad moved to touch it.

'NO! Grandad, please don't touch!' Suzy cried.

He quickly pulled his hand back. 'For goodness' sake, Suzy, I nearly jumped out of my skin! What's wrong with you?'

'I'm sorry, Grandad. I didn't mean to make you jump. But you must not touch it until we are in the mountain.'

'How do you know that?'

'I don't know; I just do. The thought jumped into my head as you went to touch it,' Suzy replied.

'I suppose I must accept what you say, especially as it's a warning,' Grandad said. 'This is certainly a very strange day and getting stranger by the minute. Thank you.' He nodded and smiled at Suzy.

'You're very welcome,' she said with a giggle.

They rested for a while, and when they started to feel a bit chilly, Grandad and Sarah looked out and noticed that they were leaving the Scottish mainland.

'We will be going over the sea very soon,' Grandad said, 'and then we'll fly across the Orkney Islands. In about another hour, we'll reach the open sea, and shortly after that, we'll be at Ogystone's island.'

Suzy put on her cold weather clothes, as she wasn't going to let herself get thoroughly frozen, and Grandad and Sarah did the same.

Suzy then sat quietly and looking out the window for a while. 'Have you noticed that the birds are no longer behind us? It's most strange. They've formed a huge circle around the army, and no matter which way you look, you can see hundreds of birds.'

'I think most of them have joined us as we've journeyed along,' Grandad replied.

As they flew over the Orkney Islands and headed out over the open sea, it became very windy, and Suzy could see hundreds of sea lions skimming through the water below, keeping pace with the army above.

Suzy then looked for land further across the sea.

We have to see it soon, she thought.

Another hour passed, and Sarah took over watching the horizon as Suzy and Grandad had a little doze in their warm clothes.

Suddenly, Sarah called, 'There it is! Straight ahead! Look, look!'

Suzy jumped up and looked out the window on the left, and Grandad looked out the window on the right. Sure enough, a dark shape loomed in the mist.

'Grandad, is that it?'

'Looks like it to me,' he said. 'I reckon we'll be there in about another thirty minutes. We'd better finish getting ourselves ready.'

Suzy felt a twinge of nervousness run through her, and then she remembered her protective shield and felt fine again. She put on her ski jacket and ski gloves, and now that she saw the snow-clad mountain, she was glad she had brought them.

They could see the island quite clearly now, and the snowy peak of the mountain poked through the fog. A few more moments passed and they were over the island, flying through the murky fog.

'Yeouw, ugh! What's that terrible smell?' Suzy said through clenched teeth.

'I hate to think,' Sarah whispered back.

Grandad, who was sitting between Sarah and Suzy, took hold of their hands and said, 'Now listen, you two. We will be landing soon, so whatever you do, make sure you stick close to the group, remember everything you've been told, and don't take any chances. I want to rescue all these little chaps, but not at the expense of losing either of you. 'And your Nan will kill me if I return without you!'

They all giggled, albeit a bit nervously.

Then, with a bump, the little house landed on a solid ledge, and the other flying machines landed all around them. Grandad brought out the box of nets, and Scratch appeared at his side.

'This way, Grandad,' Scratch called. 'Don't unload the nets yet, as we can't touch them until we are at the entrance to the tunnels.'

The humans followed Scratch along a slippery ledge, where they had to watch their footing very carefully.

'Here we are at tunnel number one,' Scratch said. 'Who's going in first?'

Grandad beckoned to Sean, the representative from Northern Ireland, along with his friends from the West Country and the Isle of Wight, and they were determined that they would go in first. Grandad opened the box and signalled to Sean to grab a net just as 150 paxteys appeared. Sean stepped back to let them go in first, and some of the paxteys at the end of the group took hold of the open end of the net and headed into the tunnel, and the rest of the paxteys supported the middle of what they realised was a giant sack, and finally, Sean and his team supported the large, empty end. As soon as the humans touched it, there was a snapping sound, time sped up, and the group disappeared into the tunnel.

'What on earth happened?' Grandad said, staring in disbelief.

'That was why I instructed you not to touch the net until it was time to use it,' Scratch explained. 'You see, the Havenley angels gave His Majesty the power of time control for this mission. Whoever touches the netting and doesn't live in this mountain will move a hundred times faster than normal whilst everything within in the mountain moves a hundred times slower. It is hoped that with this power, we will be able to get in there unseen and out so quickly that no one will be hurt. The net will work like a giant Hoover and draw in everything that has been affected by the humble weed.'

Grandad let out a low whistle and shook his head. 'If I hadn't seen it I would never have believed it. That is incredible.'

'Cool,' Suzy whispered.

'Okay, come on, then,' Grandad said. 'Let's get to the next tunnel before that Ogystone fellow finds out we're here.'

When they arrived at the next tunnel, it was time for Dougal from Scotland, Dyfed from Wales, and the groups from the Shetland Isles and the Isle of Man to go in. Just as before, 150 paxteys arrived, and half of them took the mouth of the sack and went into the tunnel, the rest of the paxteys lined themselves up along the middle of the sack, and finally the humans manoeuvred themselves around the base of the sack, gripped the net, and, *whoosh!*, they were gone.

Now it was the turn of Grandad and his group plus his friends from the New Forest and Southampton areas, Suffolk, and Norfolk.

'You all know what you have to do now,' Scratch said. 'I have to go ahead to join the King's group, which will be doing a sweep of the captives in the cells.'

'Oh, Scratch, please be careful! I wish you weren't going off on your own,' Suzy said anxiously.

'I'll only be on my own for a second. I'll be fine.' He smiled, waved, and was gone.

Grandad's group of humans watched the paxteys move into the tunnel with the front of the net, and they then spaced themselves evenly apart around the base of the net. Suzy felt a really strange sensation as if she were being lifted off her feet, and her body felt as light as a feather. However, she didn't feel as if she were moving any faster than usual.

Bump! Something hit the back of the net, and Suzy could saw a little face. It was dark and angry and glared at her, and then the paxtey it belonged to slowly closed his eyes and went to sleep.

'It's all right!' Suzy said as another one, growling and angry, was sucked into the net. 'We've come to rescue you.'

As more paxteys were dragged into the net, some screamed with fright, and all the rescuers did their best to reassure them before they fell asleep. The King had been right that some of them didn't want to be rescued, and they tried to fly away but couldn't compete with the speed of the net. Every paxtey captive was going to be rescued whether they liked it or not.

Sarah looked at all the paxteys as they flew into the net. Some were snarling and angry, others were terrified, and still others were relieved and resigned to whatever happened to them. They looked so different to what she was used to seeing. She searched frantically for her Jupee, and then she noticed one old, wrinkled, and dark face. It was difficult to see where his robes finished and his skin began. He spit with anger as he went into the depths of the net and finally landed on the part that she was holding.

'Suzy, I think I've found Jupee.' She spotted a crook in his little nose and said to Suzy, who was also staring at him, 'Jupee had a crooked nose.'

She looked closer and touched him, and although he was still growling, he calmed down.

'Jupee, is that you? It's me, Sarah.'

He growled in response, and finally, he was quiet, and he looked up at Sarah.

'Jupee, I'm here. I've come to rescue you.' Tears ran down Sarah's face. 'Oh, Jupee, don't you remember me?'

He was completely calm at last, and he turned his face and looked into her eyes. Her tears fell on him, and his eyes showed recognition. 'Sarah . . .' he whispered, and he fell asleep.

'It's him! Oh, Suzy, I've found my Jupee!'

'I'm so glad that he's safe!' Suzy said. 'Now let's get all the others.'

The group worked their way down the passageways very carefully, as the ground was stony and uneven, and they had to be so careful not to trip. The net filled up very quickly.

Suzy got quite a shock when one of the paxteys tried to chew his way out of the net. He was incredibly vicious and determined.

'Ouch!' Suzy yelled.

'Are you all right?' Grandad called.

'Yes, I'm okay, but the little beggar bit me!' As she looked back at him, he fell asleep. Then she noticed something warm on her arm. A paxtey was pouring liquid on the spot where she had been bitten.

'Can't take any chances,' he said before he dashed off.

A few more seconds passed, and then the last paxtey popped into the net as they cleared the passageway and found themselves standing in the big chamber. Before them, Ogystone sat on his stone throne screaming abuse at His Majesty and his guards.

'You think you're a ruler? Ha! You couldn't rule a troop of monkeys. In fact, you couldn't rule the fleas on monkeys!'

He stopped yelling for a moment and looked around at the whole army looking back at him. A sly smirk crossed his face. 'I stand corrected, dear brother. 'You do rule monkeys.'

The venomous words fell on deaf ears, as His Majesty was busy checking that everyone had got through the tunnel and that all the paxteys had been rescued. The guards encircled Ogystone so that he couldn't escape. So far, the plan had gone very well, except for one disappointment: the change in time hadn't affected Ogystone at all. However, the army had had the element of surprise on their side and had caught Ogystone unawares, but they hadn't been able to complete the operation without his knowledge.

Suzy let go of the net now that all the paxteys were safe, and as time returned to normal, she looked at Ogystone. She couldn't believe that something so repulsive, so cruel could ever have lived with the paxteys

Scratch appeared at her side.

'Can you believe this?' Suzy whispered to him.

'I know. I was expecting something nasty, but his looks have shocked me too,' Scratch whispered.

Ogystone shouted, 'So, Tobias, you think you've rounded everyone up, eh? Well, you haven't got everyone. The one you search for, you will never find. I've made sure of that!'

King Tobias looked across the hall at his head guard and signalled towards Ogystone. In a flash, the guard appeared at Ogystone's side, flew up, and slapped Ogystone's mouth. Ogystone gave a mighty roar, and the nasty words stopped. The guard had sealed his mouth.

Suzy slowly turned to Scratch and whispered, 'Do you think he's done something to Chamali?'

'His Majesty did say that Chamali was going to escape, but maybe he didn't. I don't know what to think now. We couldn't find him when we searched the other tunnels.'

'We have to know before we leave. Will His Majesty check for him?'

I'm going back into the tunnels to make sure, Scratch said in Suzy's head so no one else would hear.

Please be careful! Suzy answered.

Suzy then looked back at Ogystone and tried to think of what he could have done to poor Chamali. She searched his face for the answer. Then, as if he had read her thoughts, he turned to her, his evil eyes boring into hers.

You won't have Chamali; you'll never see him again! He shouted in her head.

Suzy's whole body prickled with fear, but as she continued to stare at him, she noticed something strange. Something walked right past her and into the tunnel Scratch had gone down. She looked back at the throne, but Ogystone wasn't there! She turned to the King, who was busy arranging for the rescued paxteys' journey home with his guards, and then she looked at Grandad, Sarah, and the other humans. It seemed no one had noticed Ogystone leave.

Scratch! He was on his own with Ogystone!

'Oh no!' she whispered to herself in horror. 'I have to find Scratch before he does.'

Scratch! Look out! Ogystone is coming! She called in her mind.

Ogystone had watched as all the slaves that he had worked so hard to get had been swallowed up in those sacks. If he had known about the invasion, he could have prepared for battle, but without his faithful Kerr and Kree to keep him informed, he had been beaten. This was more than he could deal with, and he had to leave, but not before he did one last thing. His face burned with rage.

'I Will Kill, Chamali! I'll show you, Tobias! You won't get everything you want today!'

He flew through the corridors with hatred in his heart and rage in his veins. He would smash his way through that shield Chamali had put up, and he would be too weak after all these weeks of starvation to put up a fight. Ogystone looked along the corridor to his left, and there it was, the door with the big *C* painted on it in the green of the humble weed. He thumped on the door and undid the bolts.

'Wake up, you miserable old storyteller. You've told your last tale. If you think you're gonna be rescued, think again!' he shouted, spitting and dribbling, his eyes glowing with evil. 'I'll make sure you never see your friends again! I'm gonna smash your snivelling, do-gooding head to a pulp!'

'No! You won't touch him!' Scratch shouted behind Ogystone.

Ogystone turned to see Scratch in such a rage that he wanted to smash this silly little pea of a paxtey. 'So you think you can stop me, do you? Let's see, shall we?'

Scratch, was hovering right in front of Ogystone's face, he was really angry as well. Unfortunately, because Scratch had allowed himself to get angry, he had dropped his protective shield.

Thud! The first thump from Ogystone sent him flying through the air, and poor Scratch crashed against the wall and fell to the floor. Ogystone then marched over and stomped on him and would have continued stomping if Suzy hadn't come round the corner at that very moment.

'No!' she shouted. 'Leave him alone!'

Suzy threw herself at Ogystone and pushed him to the floor. He was stunned for a moment but then he rose to his feet and ran at Suzy, who had laid herself over Scratch to protect him.

Ogystone thumped and kicked, but Suzy wasn't harmed, as her shield protected her.

'Keep still, Scratch. Don't move,' she whispered as the blows continued.

'You idiot human what are you doing here? Get out of my mountain!' He punched her shield.

Then, suddenly, Ogystone remembered what he was really here for and went back to unlocking Chamali's cell.

Suzy and Scratch stayed huddled on the floor as they watched. Suzy prepared herself; if Chamali was in that cell, she wasn't going to let that warty lump hurt him. He opened the door and went into the cell, but all Suzy could see was a pile of rags in the corner.

Ogystone grabbed them. Gone! He's gone! Nooo! Raaagh!'

His rage was now beyond his control and as he rose up from the ground, his body broke apart. The pieces became mist and evaporated up through the rocks and out into the air. The mist then floated across the land to the sea and finally settled into the sea.

Suzy and Scratch sat there for a few moments in disbelief, watching to make sure that he wasn't going to come back.

'Scratch, we must check that cell,' Suzy said. She jumped up and ran into the cell.

'He isn't here,' Suzy said. 'I think he did escape just as His Majesty said he would.'

Suzy came out and looked at Scratch. He struggled to get up, as his wings were broken, and his arm seemed to be damaged, too.

'Oh no Scratch your badly hurt, don't move! Come on, it's my turn to take care of you.' Suzy gently picked him up and carried him back to the throne room, where everyone was glad to see them, as they had wondered where they had gone. Grandad was about to come looking for them. Ogystone's apparition was no longer on the throne.

Grandad rushed forward to help Suzy, but she stopped him. 'It's all right, Grandad. I'll carry Scratch.'

Grandad gave her an understanding look and stepped out of her way.

The humans and paxteys then prepared the sacks containing their special cargo to go home. Suzy planned for Scratch to travel home in little house with her so he could stay with her and Nan and Grandad until he was better.

When everyone was outside and way up in the air, ready for the journey home, King Tobias circled them on Bira and addressed them.

'It's over at last. The evil has gone. We can all have our lives and our lands back, thanks to you, all of you, to your bravery and your courage. I am proud to know you all and to be able to call you my friends. Now let's go home!' He waved his arms and a bright light flashed across the army, and they all moved as one. All Suzy could see below the little house was a bright blue light flashing by at an incredible speed, yet inside the little house, everything felt normal, and they seemed to be flying at their normal speed. Scratch said that the angels had given the King the choice of going at this speed on the way to the mountain or coming back, and he had chosen it for coming back.

In just a few minutes, the little house landed in Grandad's back garden. Nan and Julie ran up the garden path to them.

'At last, we've been so worried,' Nan said.

'We're fine. We all made it back,' Grandad responded. 'Just get that old kettle on. I'm dying for a cuppa!'

Suzy climbed out of the little house last with her dear friend Scratch in her arms. She looked at the little house and patted it fondly. 'Oh thank you, dear little house you can rest now that the mission is over.' She then looked down at Scratch. 'Come on, Scratch, let's get you home and comfortable.'

She smiled, and he gave her a weak smile in return. She then noticed a mist swirling around her, as she carried on up the path as quickly as possible to get Scratch in out of the dampness. When she looked down again, Scratch had disappeared from her arms, and then she looked up, and the house was gone, too!

'What's happening? Where's everyone gone?'

Suzy found herself sitting on the bench on the cliff, looking out to sea. She was back in 2027. She had been miles away, and she shook her head to pull herself together.

'Wow! For a while there it felt as if I was really back there all those years ago.'

She smiled to herself. What a joy it was to remember that time full of adventure, sadness, and happiness back in 2002.

Lightning Source UK Ltd.
Milton Keynes UK
UKOW05f0730190114

224847UK00003B/162/P